OVER THE RAINBOW

TRINITY LAKES ROMANCE

BOOK EIGHT

MEREDITH RESCE

Golden Grain Publishing

Over the Rainbow

Book 8 – Trinity Lakes Romance series

Copyright © 2024 Meredith Resce

Golden Grain Publishing
PO Box 880 Unley SA 5061

 A catalogue record for this book is available from the National Library of Australia

978-0-6489537-9-1 — eBook

978-0-6459094-0-1 — Paperback

This is a work of fiction. Names, characters and incidents are either the product of the author's imagination or are used fictitiously, and any resemblance to actual events or persons, living or dead, is entirely coincidental.

Scriptures taken from the Holy Bible, New International Version®, NIV®. Copyright © 1973, 1978, 1984, 2011 by Biblica, Inc.™ Used by permission of Zondervan. All rights reserved worldwide. www.zondervan.com The "NIV" and "New International Version" are trademarks registered in the United States Patent and Trademark Office by Biblica, Inc.™

Cover Art by Annie Millard Designs

❀ Created with Vellum

CHAPTER ONE

Arianne Rayne inhaled a deep breath of determination. This was going to be hard. Possibly not as hard as the day they'd given her the news. And probably not as hard as that day when Gavin had decided to cut and run. But hard nonetheless.

"Are you set?" Arianne's father put her suitcase on the airport trolley next to his.

"Where are Gran and Pa going to meet us?"

"I told them to go to the passenger pickup zone—save them paying for a park."

Arianne placed her hands on the wheels of her chair. Thank goodness Dad was allowing her the independence of moving herself around. It had taken forever to get through to him that she needed to develop confidence in doing for herself. She'd had to accept help, getting Dad to transfer her from the plane seat into the airport wheelchair, finding the elevator and getting to the ground floor. But now she had her own wheelchair, she felt capable of following him out to the passenger pickup zone.

Several months ago, she wouldn't have thought twice about access for those with a disability. What a difference a few months made. And what a journey she'd been on trying to adjust, not just to the new physical limitations, but to her emotions.

"Uh-oh!"

Arianne looked up to see what had attracted Dad's interest. Gran and Pa were running—literally running—towards them, Gran's arms outstretched, and it wasn't hard to see the emotion brewing on her face. *Don't make a scene, please.* She had been the center of so many scenes in the last months that she could have staged a Broadway musical.

"Ari." Gran reached them and bent to her level, throwing strong, loving arms around her. She was sobbing. So much for not making a scene. The last time Arianne had seen her grandparents had been shortly after the accident, while she was still in the San Francisco hospital recovering from the initial decompression surgery. That was almost four months ago. At the time, everyone had been in shock at the prognosis, and Gran had been the most controlled out of all the family. Judging by her crushing embrace, it seemed she may have been saving her emotion for now.

"Move along, Mother." Pa stood, waiting for his turn. "So glad to see you, darling girl."

Pa's hug was less like a boa constrictor but communicated the same amount of love.

"I thought we agreed to meet you in the pickup zone." Dad motioned the party towards the exit doors.

"I couldn't just leave you to wait on the side of the pavement," Gran said. "We've been anticipating your arrival for so long. You needed a proper welcome." Gran put her hand on Arianne's shoulder as they moved toward the exit. Thank goodness Gran didn't feel the need to push her. Perhaps it was unreasonable to expect everyone to understand, but after months of being literally dependent on other people, Arianne needed to know that she could function independently—or at least be on the way to functioning independently.

Arianne had a portable disability placard to use the accessible parking space, but Gran and Pa didn't have it, so they had to go the extra distance to where their SUV was parked. When it came to transferring from chair to car, Arianne knew she wouldn't be able to do it yet. She had practiced building upper body strength, and had seen how she could use a transfer sliding board to maneuver into the vehicle, but she needed more strength and more training for it to be safe. She would need her father's assistance again.

"Can I do it?" Pa asked when they reached the SUV. "I'd like to learn how to help properly."

Arianne nodded. Pa wasn't an old man—well, he was in his late sixties, but he was a farmer, and his fitness and strength were the same as they'd always been. He was capable of lifting her from the chair to the front seat of the car.

"Thanks, Pa." Arianne hurried to reach for her seatbelt before Pa felt the need to buckle her in.

The two-and-a-half-hour drive from Spokane to Trinity Lakes was uneventful. The grown-ups—despite being twenty-four, her grandparents and father were the grown-ups—chatted about life on the farm, Dad's job in the city, and the comings and goings in Trinity Lakes, the town where Dad grew up. Arianne noticed they didn't talk about her and her new life challenges.

Yes, challenges. Despite the information she'd received from various people-with-disability groups, who encouraged her to embrace the idea that she was a whole person, she was not at that place mentally. At this stage, she still saw herself as having challenges that she would have to learn to deal with. As would those who were close to her. A new stage in life. She was now a person with a disability.

———

MATTHEW KENNEDY CHECKED his phone for the fifth time that afternoon. It was early morning in Australia. Surely Jane would text him today.

"Cut it out, would you, bro?" His sister, Lucy, nudged him with her foot.

Matthew looked up from his phone and glared.

"What?" Lucy shrugged innocently. "If she texts you, you'll hear the ding."

Matthew wanted to deny he'd been waiting for a text, but it was no use. Lucy knew him and she knew about his long-distance friendship—a friendship he hoped would develop into a relationship on the same continent.

"Why don't you call Elissa? She'll know if there's something up with her sister."

Lucy was apparently more concerned about his lovelorn state than he'd guessed. He watched as she dialed a number and held out her phone to him.

Elissa's name was on the screen, and he looked at the phone like it was a rattlesnake. "What are you doing?" He couldn't stop the panic in his voice.

"I'm putting you out of your misery. It's a perfectly good Sunday afternoon, and all you can do is mope around." She gave another small thrust of the phone in his direction, her eyebrows raised in a no-nonsense expression.

"Fine." If he didn't take it, who knew what Lucy would say about him to Elissa. He took the phone and held it to his ear.

"Hi, Lucy." It was Liam's voice on the other end of the call. "Elissa's out riding with Georgia at the moment. She left her phone behind."

"It's Matt." This was a stupid way to start a phone call—him calling Liam on Elissa's phone, using Lucy's phone.

"Oh, hey, Matt. Do you want me to have Elissa call you back?"

Stupider and stupider. He hadn't made the call in the first place.

"No. Don't worry. Lucy thought it might help if I asked Elissa if Jane was okay."

"Jane?" There was surprise in Liam's voice.

"Yeah. I mean, we've been texting since she went back to Australia, but I haven't heard from her in nearly four weeks. I was getting a bit worried."

"Right." What was that tone in Liam's voice?

"Is she okay?" Matthew could feel his tone squeaking, like he was an anxious teenage boy.

There was a prolonged pause on the other end, which added to his anxiety. Had something happened to Jane? Was she all right?

"Aah … Matt …"

Matthew's uncertainty ramped up to maximum, but he couldn't say anything over the lump in his throat. All moisture had disappeared from his mouth.

"Listen, I'm not sure I'm supposed to say anything, but Jane's …"

"What's happened?" Matthew couldn't cope with Liam's slow delivery. "Has she been hurt?"

"No. Not at all." This was good news, but Liam's tone was still strained. "Look, buddy, I hate to be the one to tell you this, but Jane's going to announce her engagement this weekend."

The bottom fell out of Matthew's stomach leaving a gaping hole through which cold air rushed in.

"I told Elissa we should have told you, but she didn't seem to think there was anything serious between you and Jane."

What could he say? There wasn't anything serious—well, formally serious. He'd enjoyed the time they'd spent together last year and they'd continued to text with occasional video calls over the months. Had he entertained serious intentions? His brother, Caleb, had followed his heart to Australia. While that had turned out well for him, had Matthew been prepared to do the same? Had he been prepared to give up his family and life in Trinity Lakes?

"Matt? Are you okay?" Liam sounded worried.

"We weren't serious, but I'd hoped … you know …"

"If it's any consolation, her fiancé is her first boyfriend. It hadn't gone anywhere because Charles's family didn't approve of Jane. They'd made things difficult in the past."

"So they approve now?"

Liam laughed. "Not hardly. But Charles has done well for himself in business, and Jane applied for a position in his new company."

Matthew closed his eyes against the tight ball in his chest. He knew Lucy was watching him, trying to read into every word he said, every expression. He didn't know what was hurting more, his heart or his pride.

"Netherfield Educational Systems is the business. Jane is working in the training and development department, and their relationship is back on track. Elissa is really happy for them, even if his family isn't."

"Right." Matthew should say he was glad, or happy for them, or offer well-wishes, but it felt like a betrayal. The relationship he'd imagined building with Jane had reached dizzying heights of satisfaction, while apparently she'd hardly given him a second thought. A fun vacation romance fizzled to nothing.

"I'm sorry, Matt. I hope it was okay to tell you."

Too late now. And better to know than keep chasing rainbows. "Don't worry about it. Pass on my regards when you're next talking to her." They were the right words to say, but they sounded hollow in his ears.

He ended the call and handed the phone back to Lucy without looking her in the eye. She wasn't going to be left out and chased his gaze around until they connected.

"What did he say?"

"She's engaged to her old boyfriend," he finally said. "Happy?"

To his surprise, Lucy's face fell. "Oh." Then she bit her lip, looking slightly guilty. "I'm sorry, bro. I just thought it would be better if you knew for sure."

"Mmm." He went to the fridge and surveyed the contents, giving himself a moment to avoid her scrutiny.

"Did she ever give you the impression that she was hoping for something permanent?" Lucy peered over his shoulder as he grabbed bagels and cream cheese. "I know you had a great time when she was here, but it's been a year since she went back to Australia. It wasn't like Caleb and Alanah. Was it?"

Matthew slammed the ingredients on the kitchen counter with unnecessary force. Lucy came up behind him and handed him a jar of dill pickles. His sister knew him well. Nothing like cream cheese and pickles on a bagel for comfort food.

Lucy lay her head on his shoulder. "Let's eat our weight in junk food and watch some hockey."

That sounded like the best plan for a broken heart. Diversion. With any luck, they'd catch Mitchell Reilly throw down the gloves and beat the tar out of his opponent.

———

TRINITY LAKES. At last, a place where Arianne could rest and bask in the memories of childhood.

"Do you remember the adventure camps you and your brothers used to come to over the summer?" Gran seemed pleased to have found something not-awkward to say as they drove past the sign pointing to the Trinity Lakes Summer Campground. And she was right.

"Some of my best memories are around summer camps." Canoeing, tree-climbing, swimming, sitting around the campfire singing. Just seeing the lakes as they drove into town sent all the warm fuzzies into a swirl.

Why had everyone gone silent again? Oh, right. All the fun of physical activity, and she with two legs that she could hardly get to move.

"Listen, Gran and Pa, let's have that frank discussion right now."

"Ari." There was the predictable caution in Dad's voice. He was always trying to avoid the subject, one of the reasons she'd decided to leave San Francisco and come back to her favorite childhood setting.

"Okay, so Dad struggles with candid examination of my newly acquired condition. Sorry, Dad." She cast a weak smile over her shoulder in his direction. The sad look of worry didn't leave his face. "But I'm counting on you two to face the situation squarely and not shy away from the hard facts. It is as it is, and this awkward silence is going to drive me up the wall. I came here because I want to deal with the new me, and I want your support to do it."

"Don't hold back what you really think, my dear." Gran's blunt response from the back seat was confirmation that this was where she needed to be.

"In Dad's defense, I haven't always dealt with how I feel in a sensible way." Arianne recalled several self-pity-soaked outbursts that saw her friends shrink back and eventually stop visiting. Regret knifed her inside. They hadn't understood, but she hadn't been patient with them either. Her frustrated accusations still rang in her ears as something she wished she could call back. However, dodging reality and walking about on eggshells wasn't the way forward either. Denial was her mother's superpower. Arianne needed an environment where she could wrestle with the new conditions openly and honestly and find a way to live. Truly live.

"I don't want to discard some of the best memories of my life just because it hurts to remember I can't run in the egg and spoon race anymore. In fact, I might sign up as a counselor for the next summer camp."

"Ari. Please." Dad had never been able to cope with her straightforward approach. Both parents were great at support—if support meant cotton wool and guarded conversation.

"Do you want to stop at the Bellbird Café for lunch?" Pa's question might have been designed to change the subject.

"It's probably best if we head straight to the farm and get Ari settled in." Dad was quick to answer.

"I'd love to stop, but Dad's probably right. Let's come into town and have lunch soon." Arianne relaxed in her seat and continued to enjoy the memories of many childhood visits.

"Don't you just love coming back home?" She looked to her father, who was also gazing out the window. How did he feel about the passing quaintness, from the friendly welcome sign, the poplars planted either side of the road, to Main Street with an eclectic range of stores, guarded by vintage streetlamps? The sun glinting off Lake Wainscott. The park in front, where Becky's Coffee Cart was set up. So many memories of kayaking and playing in the park, then rushing off to get a chocolate shake from Joe's Diner. "Such good times."

Dad gave a sigh.

"What?" Arianne challenged.

"This hasn't been home since I left for college."

"More's the pity." Arianne didn't miss Gran's comment from behind. Was that disappointment or anger in her tone?

"I wasn't cut out to be a farmer." There was definite defensiveness in Dad's comment.

Arianne checked for Pa's reaction. His jaw tightened. It must have been hard, having a son who showed no interest in the family heritage. Well, she was here now. Unless a random cousin popped up out of nowhere, she was ready to show all the interest in the world. Like it or not, Trinity Lakes and the farm were the only constants in her life, and she planned to engage with her roots. No more being dragged from place to place while her parents chased careers and promotions. Knowing her parents, they wouldn't stay in San Francisco forever. One thing was for certain. They were unlikely to come back and settle here.

Driving through town and then the four miles out to the farm was a warm homecoming, with trees like old friends waving a cheerful welcome. Mom had never liked the trip to Trinity Lakes. Their twice-yearly visits seemed to be more out of obligation on Dad's part, with no enthusiasm from Mom. The opposite. Constant complaints about the distance, the country, the flies, the dirt, the animals. Mom was a city girl, and once she'd got Dad, she was determined he would be a city person as well. Gran and Pa's love and kindness were the thing that drew Arianne and her brothers, and Dad managed to hold sway in the decision. Otherwise, they might never have visited.

"Wow! The Darcys must be coming up in the world." Dad watched as they passed the elaborate gated entrance to a long tree-lined drive.

"The grandson, Liam, has done very well for himself. He's an entrepreneur," Pa said.

"No farming for him then?"

"They farm horses, sheep and solar panels," Gran answered.

"Solar panels? Really?" Arianne's interest was piqued. She had taken a course on renewable energy as part of her college major.

"It's all new and fangled," Pa said. "Can't see it being of any real use in the future."

"That's what they said about the automobile when it was first invented." Arianne smiled.

It was lunchtime by the time they arrived at the family farm. The dogs ran to the end of their tethers, barking excitedly.

"Silly dogs," Gran said.

"They're welcoming you home, aren't they?" The two border collies stood at the garden gate entrance, still barking.

"I suppose that must be it."

"Or they're stupid," Pa said. "I've tried to teach them, but they go mad every time a vehicle approaches."

"Even a vehicle they know?" Dad betrayed his interest.

"Especially a vehicle they know." Pa pulled the SUV up in front of the garden gate, crunching the handbrake into position.

"Well there, you see," Arianne smiled as she opened her door. "They're obviously ecstatic to see you home."

Everyone undid their seatbelts and opened car doors, but only Arianne was left, unable to disembark. She picked her stubborn legs up one at a time and turned herself out, ready for someone to lift her. Pa arrived first. He was a gruff old fellow, but his heart of gold couldn't stay hidden. Arianne watched him assess the angles and obstacles.

"Ready for a ride?" he asked.

"No horsing around today, Pa. I'm not eight years old anymore."

Dad pulled her chair from the back of the vehicle, unfolded it, and set it on the ground, ready to go.

"We'll sort out some way to have us some fun later." Pa leaned forward and she put her arms around his neck. He lifted her down and allowed gravity to assist as she settled into her chair. It had been hard at first, accepting that someone needed to help her transfer in certain situations, but Pa used to pick her up and fling her around when she was a child as part of their rough and tumble play. This was sort of like that. Sort of. Except he was strong and gentle, and ensured her spine was supported. It was going to be all right. Mom and Dad had tried to deter her from moving to Trinity Lakes, citing doubt about Gran and Pa's ability to cope. Arianne searched for her father's gaze and tried to inject as much reassurance as she could into her smile.

The driveway was rough gravel, and it would take extra

muscle to power her chair across to the paved garden path—muscle power she didn't have in her right shoulder. The scapula injury was healed but by no means rehabilitated. Dad grabbed the rear handles and started pushing.

On a smooth surface, Arianne would have objected. Today she was going to have to accept help. Still. "Dad ..."

"Not today, Ari. Let's get you settled first, and then you can give your lectures about independence."

Arianne swallowed her feelings. She hadn't been going to object—this time—despite how she hated her helplessness. Gran was observing closely.

"Go on. Spit it out." Gran could always tell.

"I hate condescension and pity."

"Good to know." Pa walked past, carrying her two suitcases.

"Go easy on your father, Ari. He's only trying to make things easier for you." Gran was her usual forthright self.

"I'll eventually have to learn to manage on my own." Arianne wasn't ready to yield to her powerless status.

"That you will, and we will have to learn right along with you. Just give us some time to understand and adjust. Would that be all right?"

Why did she feel like Gran had just scolded her? Perhaps she had. Was she being unreasonable with Dad? A quick reflection indicated that perhaps she had been. Her regret over how she'd pushed her friends away underscored Gran's point. They were all learning. She needed to have some grace as well.

The garden was beautiful, the spring flowers a colorful display in all the garden beds, and the fruit trees in full blossom and budding leaf. Thank goodness she had escaped the city, especially that cold, clinical rehabilitation center. Life here would be so much better.

And then she faced the porch steps—five of them.

Before she'd had time to express her dismay, Pa had grabbed

the front of her chair, and in cooperation with Dad, they soon had her sailing through the air and onto the porch.

"That's at the top of my to-do list," Pa said, as he let her gently down.

"What?" Dad asked.

"To build a proper access ramp so Ari can come and go as she pleases."

The urge to throw herself into her grandfather's arms was upon her, but still her legs had no interest in cooperating.

"She wants a hug," Gran said. She was so in tune, that woman. So unlike Mom.

Then, miracle of miracles, Pa bent down and let her hug him. He was not one who could ever be described as demonstrative, but today, he'd hugged her twice.

Momentous happenings.

CHAPTER TWO

"Where are you going?" Lucy grabbed Matthew's arm as he took a sharp turn.

"I need to use the bathroom." It was a lie—or perhaps not. He needed the bathroom to hide in. Thankfully, Lucy didn't argue but let him go on his way through the church foyer. It was stupid. He knew it, but he couldn't seem to help himself. How embarrassing that he should have been so obvious about his feelings for Jane, only to find out it had been a meaningless vacation romance, ended by her return to Australia. Properly ended by her getting engaged to her old boyfriend. Seeing Jane's sister, Elissa, in the church foyer had hit him hard. Was it embarrassment? Was it hurt? Could you get hurt from such a light association? It was ridiculous, that's what.

The exterior door to the bathroom opened, and Matthew turned to the sink and turned the faucet. It wasn't a good look being caught brooding in the loo. Funny he should revert to the Aussie term he'd used as a teenager when he'd lived Down Under for those years.

"Hey, mate." Speaking of Aussies, Adam Lancaster walked in.

"Hey." This was awkward. No. It wasn't awkward. He was washing his hands. Nothing extraordinary to see here.

"I'm glad I caught you," Adam said. "Can I chat to you after the service?"

"Sure." At least Adam didn't want to chat right here. That was something girls did, heading off to the bathroom in packs and coming back talking and laughing.

With someone else in the bathroom, Matthew couldn't hide anymore. Surely Elissa and Liam would have left the foyer by now.

He wasn't back in the foyer for two seconds before Lucy came to his side. "Are you avoiding the Darcys?" His sister had him pegged. Typical Lucy. She could spot a motive at ten paces. "What are you worried about?" Her nonchalance was unnerving. "Nobody knows."

Knows? "What do you mean, nobody knows? Knows what?"

Lucy laughed and continued to head to the sanctuary.

"Luce." Matthew hurried after her. He would lose the opportunity if they entered the reverent atmosphere. "What do you mean?"

"Nobody knows you were in love with Jane Bennett," she whispered. "Stop being strange. Act normal."

Strange? Act normal? If he was self-conscious before, he was more so now. Lucy thought he was being abnormally strange— like more strange than usual. As they searched for a place to sit, Lucy led the way toward where the Darcys were sitting. Matthew grabbed her arm and tugged her towards the opposite side of the church. So, he was self-conscious. He needed some time to settle his ruffled emotions before being comfortable around Jane's family.

"Look. The Raynes' granddaughter is here." Lucy walked straight up to the young woman sitting in a wheelchair in the space designated for the disabled. Her grandparents, Jolly and Ruth Rayne, were seated next to her. Matthew froze. Ever since that incident with Mr. Searle, he'd always felt anxious around people in wheelchairs. Some might call it an unreasonable fear, but his four-year-old self hadn't known not to stare. And certainly hadn't known that the gruff old amputee would berate him for his childish question. *What's wrong with your leg, Mister?* Matthew shuddered at the memory. *You're a horrible child and I hope your mother punishes you.* His mother hadn't punished him, but she'd given him a long, serious talk that felt like a punishment. He'd learned a big lesson that day. Keep out of the way, and don't ask stupid questions.

"This is my brother, Matt." Lucy stood aside and pushed him forward. "Matt, this is Arianne Rayne. She's new to town."

"Hello." Matthew shifted his feet and looked longingly at the other side of the church. It would have been easier for him to sit right next to Elissa and Liam.

"Hey." The woman spoke to him, but she turned her face forward straight away. Good job. The only experience he'd had with this kind of thing had been traumatic for all involved, and he had a strong urge to escape. The fact he still felt this way shamed him. But with his emotions already frayed, it felt like he was tiptoeing on a fast-unravelling tightrope, and any second, he'd fall.

Thankfully, Lucy charged off to find a seat and he followed. Lucy's ramrod straight head and shoulders, suggested she was angry with him. There was no figuring out the inner workings of a sister's mind. By the time he'd sat down, he could practically see the steam pouring from her ears.

"What's wrong?"

"How could you, Matt?" Even in a whisper, her anger was obvious.

"How could I what?"

Lucy gave him a first-class glare that would have melted any other man. But he was her brother. He'd faced the Lucy glare before. He usually knew what the problem was. This time, he had no clue. But it was too late. The band had taken to the stage and Alex Sinclair was opening in prayer. Time to focus on worship.

———

ARIANNE FOUGHT BACK TEARS. This was her first outing in Trinity Lakes. Why had she held such high hopes of being welcomed and connecting? Right from when they'd first entered the parking lot, the disappointments had started. There were only two disabled access parking spaces, and they were both in use by the time they'd arrived.

"That'll be some of the older church members," Gran had said.

Pa had sniffed. There had been no parking placards displayed on their rearview mirrors. It seemed he doubted the legitimate need to use the access parks. This had been a blow to her plans of independent living. Her complicated shoulder and scapula fracture had only just healed enough for her to start propelling herself—and then only on smooth surfaces. Pa had needed to go right to the farthest part of the parking lot to find enough space for her to transfer straight to her wheelchair. The closer conventional parking spots did not have enough room. This part of the parking lot wasn't paved. There had been no chance of her propelling herself over this uneven gravel surface.

"Do you want a push, Ari?" Pa had asked.

"Thanks, Pa." Arianne had choked back the lump that had been clogging her throat. Just like the farmyard, independent movement was impossible in these conditions.

Then the entrance. Yes, the church had allocated accessible parking, but hadn't thought through the steps. Only two, but really, there should have been a ramp. She wasn't strong enough to get her chair up one step, never mind two. How on earth did the elderly in this church manage? She'd watched as an older lady using a walker had waited for assistance to get up the steps. Everyone was eager to assist. But Arianne wasn't an old lady. She was twenty-four and planned to live an independent life— as much as she could.

This first excursion into her new community was only half an hour in, and already she was frustrated by the access issues. And then there was that horrible introduction to Matt whatever-his-name-was. She'd only seen him for five seconds and could tell he was looking everywhere in the room except her and was in a hurry to move on. At least his sister seemed nice and friendly...

Tears stung her eyes. As the worship music swelled and the voices of the congregation joined in, Arianne closed her eyes and squeezed tears away. Whether it was here or in San Francisco, she was going to have to face the barriers against inclusion. Her counsellors had gently warned her, and now she was beginning to understand. She didn't want other people to pity her so she needed to resist self-pity, because at times like this, self-pity sat on her shoulder shouting out all kinds of reasons why she should go home and never venture out again.

It was hard pushing through. The music was familiar, but sometimes the words seemed trite. Songs like *You are Good* and *Your Mercy Never Fails*. Arianne could agree mentally, but her heart wasn't satisfied.

Why me? God, why didn't You prevent the accident?

By the end of service, Arianne steeled herself. She wanted to make friends. She wanted to find a place where she belonged. Sliding back into the grief and depression that had shadowed the past months was not going to help her cause.

"Do you want me to stay with you?" Gran was watching someone on the other side of the sanctuary.

"Do you have someone you need to see?" It seemed obvious by her body language.

"Marianne Kennedy. I'm part of the Australian Festival committee, and just want to check a few details with her."

"Go on. I'll be fine with Pa."

But by the time Gran had stepped away, Pa had been collared by another man and they were deep in conversation about crops and the likelihood of rain.

It was time to take the bull by the horns—or chair by the wheels. She wasn't going to make meaningful connections by waiting for people to come to her. She saw the girl she'd met earlier, near the door. Here went nothing.

"Hi, again." Arianne rolled up to Lucy.

"Oh, hey." Lucy smiled confidently. "Did you enjoy the service?"

It wasn't time to be honest about internal struggles. They'd only just met. Surface chitchat was going to have to do.

"It was lovely."

"How long will you be staying with your grandparents?"

"At this stage, it's a permanent move. I haven't got anything going on anywhere else."

Lucy looked concerned. Had Arianne been oversharing?

"What about your parents?" Lucy asked.

"They're in San Francisco." They didn't need her, and she was coping better without their cloistered method of care. But that would be oversharing.

"Do you have any siblings?" Lucy asked.

"I have two brothers, both younger than me and at college out of state."

"I have two brothers and two sisters." No matter how stilted the flow, Lucy seemed willing to persist.

"I met your brother Matt, earlier, didn't I?"

"I'm sorry about him. He was a bit rude, but honestly, he's not really like that."

"Don't worry about it. I'm getting used to it."

"Used to it?"

Whoops. Self-pity alert. "A lot of people don't really know what to say or how to act when they meet someone with a disability."

"Oh." Lucy looked like she was trying to find something to say. Point proven right there.

"It's okay if you have someone else you need to talk to."

"What?" Lucy seemed alarmed. "No. Sorry. I'm one of those lots of people."

"What?"

"I don't know what to say or how to act. I'm really sorry."

A warm-fuzzy feeling washed through Arianne's heart. "Don't worry about it. That was me last year, before the accident. Being without the use of one's legs teaches you a whole range of new things."

Lucy smiled. "You know what, I think I could learn a lot from you. Would you like to go out to lunch?"

"Absolutely." An offer of friendship. Sure, Lucy was a bit clumsy about how she talked, but it wasn't like there was a club for people with disabilities in town. If she was going to make friends, it was going to be with "able" people. Already Lucy seemed to be open to learning and understanding. That was promising.

"Do you have your own wheels?" Even as the words came out of Lucy's mouth she stopped, her eyes wide with a look of horror. "I'm so sorry, Arianne. I didn't mean ..."

Arianne laughed. She had to. It was time to make friends, not get offended by people who had no idea. "I know what you mean, Lucy." She tapped her tires. "Other than these, I don't have wheels. I could get Gran and Pa to drop me somewhere, unless you'd be willing to give me a ride."

Lucy's eyes remained wide, and the horror switched to worry.

"I can coach you how to make it happen. It should be okay."

"But how do you get from the chair into the car?"

"Right." Dad and Pa had been her help so far. Arianne hoped that once her shoulder gained strength and movement, she would master the transfer … if she was in a low hatchback. But as of today, she was still as weak as a kitten on her right side. Besides, she didn't know what sort of vehicle Lucy drove. "I can get Pa to drop me. Where do you want to go?"

Before Lucy had a chance to answer, her brother approached. "Hey, Luce." He remained a few feet away and didn't acknowledge Arianne. "You okay if we go to the lake for lunch?"

"Excuse me a minute." Lucy closed the gap between her and her brother and turned her back. Arianne tried not to listen, but her hearing was great, even if her mobility wasn't.

"I just asked Arianne to join us for lunch."

"What?" Even at a distance, she could hear panic in Matt's tone. Great. Awesome way to make the new person feel welcome. "No. She can't come. The others want to play volley-ball and stuff after lunch."

"Matt." There was distinct warning in Lucy's tone which did nothing to soothe the pain of being pushed aside that sliced into Arianne's gut.

"Hey, Lucy," Arianne called. "Don't worry about it. Go with the others. I'm fine." She injected as much cheer and couldn't-care-less into her tone as she could muster, and schooled her chin muscles to hold firm, despite the fact they wanted to give way to the emotion that had gripped her throat.

Lucy turned back and away from her brother. She was flushed. Embarrassed or angry? "I'm really sorry, Arianne." Her jaw was clenched. She was angry with her brother. Well, good. At least that justified some of the horrible feelings pushing at the back of her eyes, threatening to come gushing out.

"Don't worry about it." Arianne fought hard to maintain a light airy tone. It took a supersonic amount of self-control.

"Can I have your number?" Lucy asked, pulling out her cell phone poised ready to type.

Arianne held out her hand. "I'll type it in."

"I'll call soon to make a proper arrangement that my brother can't thoughtlessly wreck." Lucy took her phone back. "I'm so upset with him, I could spit."

Arianne laughed. "Don't do that. At least, not in the church sanctuary."

———

THAT WAS EMBARRASSING. Matthew walked back into the church foyer. It wasn't that he didn't want to be friendly, but this made him anxious. What was Lucy thinking? How did she think they were supposed to manage looking after someone in a wheelchair? He already doubted that he could talk to the girl, let alone anything else. He scanned the folks still milling about in conversation and saw Adam Lancaster. Right. He was supposed to catch up with Adam about something.

"Hey, mate." Adam reached out to shake Matthew's hand. "I heard you're working up at the Country Club gym now."

"Yeah. Been there a few months, since I finished that personal training course."

"I'm wondering if you can help me with one of my physio clients. I've made up a specific rehabilitation training plan with special exercises, but as you know, I work from home and my client needs to work in a gym at least three or four times a week. She's going to need support."

"That should be fine. Between me and Jeannette, we should be able to fit her in. Email me the plan and I'll go over it with Jeannette."

"Great. There are hydrotherapy classes at the country club as well, yeah? I assume they're part of the gym facility."

Matthew nodded. "Yes. We have classes several times a week.

Usually for older people. We sometimes get another instructor for that."

"Right. Perhaps you can help my client work through some routines in the water when the pool is free."

"Shouldn't be a problem. Email me the details and we'll sort it out."

"That's great, mate. Thanks." Adam clapped him on the shoulder. "I see Lucy has already welcomed her, which is awesome. She's new to town."

Matthew froze. The only new person Lucy had welcomed was the young woman in the wheelchair. Surely Adam didn't mean her? Should she even be at a normal gym? Surely she would need specialist care. But he didn't get the chance to ask as Adam had retreated with his wife, Lauren, and they were leaving the church. Perhaps Adam meant someone else. He hoped so. Honestly, the idea of working with someone in a wheelchair terrified him. He would be sure to say or do the wrong thing and besides, he wasn't qualified.

"Come on." Lucy approached, but didn't stop, only giving the terse command as she moved outside.

"What's your hurry?" Matthew extended his stride to keep up. "Lucy?" She didn't answer but got in the passenger side of his truck. "What is your problem?" He didn't try to hide his annoyance as he got in the driver's side.

"Matthew Kennedy!"

Uh oh. She'd turned into his mother using his full name. "What?"

"I have never been so mortified in my entire life."

"What are you talking about?"

"I've never seen you act in such an unkind, thoughtless way."

"Unkind? Thoughtless? What are you talking about?"

"Really? Fine. Stop the truck. I'll get a lift home with Mom and Dad."

"Fine!" He pulled the truck over about fifty yards from the church parking lot entrance.

"You should apologize." Lucy glared at him as she opened the truck door.

"For what?"

"Honestly? You really don't know how awful you were to Arianne back there?"

"Arianne? Who's Arianne?"

"Argh!" Lucy climbed out of the truck and slammed the door.

"Who's Arianne?" Matthew called. "If I was rude, I'd like to apologize."

"Arianne, who I invited to lunch, who you blew off."

"The girl in the wheelchair?" A chill ran through his system. How on earth were they supposed to help her? They could easily do something to make things worse.

"How can you be so clueless? Arianne is a person with feelings, just like you and me."

The cold sensation iced his veins. This young woman wasn't Mr. Searle. She hadn't barked at him angrily—yet. Regret tickled his conscience into life. He didn't want to hurt anyone's feelings. Would never, if he could help it. But this situation was something he wasn't trained to deal with. He didn't know what to do.

"Well?" Lucy stood on the pavement glaring back in the truck at him.

"It's not something I know how to cope with, Luce. You have to understand."

"Understand? How about you exercise some common decency. All you had to do was be polite."

"Luce ..."

"How about finding some empathy and trying to understand it from Arianne's point of view?"

Matthew took a deep breath. Once his sister decided to

defend someone, she meant business. He was chagrined to think his distance could have been interpreted as rudeness.

"Look, I'm sorry. I didn't mean to be rude, but she's only visiting her grandparents and will only be here for a short time anyway. She probably didn't notice."

"Oooh!" Lucy slammed the door in his face.

The girl wouldn't have noticed, would she? He had a horrible feeling that perhaps she had noticed, and he had just presented himself as … what? Hopefully Lucy was overreacting.

CHAPTER THREE

A new day, a new opportunity to engage with her new community. Arianne's physical therapist had recommended a heap of different exercises, some to strengthen her upper body, particularly for the right side that had lost condition from the shoulder injury. Other exercises designed to try to establish new neural pathways and perhaps coax some of her still-connected nerves to engage. The doctors had said her spinal cord injury was an incomplete injury below L5. While she couldn't walk at this stage, there was a possibility of getting some mobility as the still connected nerves registered the need for use. The beauty of neuroplasticity.

With her paper copy of the exercise program tucked in her shoulder bag, Arianne wheeled out of her ground-floor bedroom into the kitchen.

"Are you looking forward to the gym session?" Gran asked, after they'd said grace.

"I've always loved training and exercise, particularly during basketball season." Arianne pulled up at the kitchen table and took some toast from the rack.

"You had hopes of making a professional team, didn't you?" Pa was sipping his morning coffee.

Arianne laughed. "I was never going to make it professionally, but I was enjoying reaching as high as I could go in college basketball."

"Do you think you'll redirect that energy into a new sport with wheels?" Pa asked.

"Jolly! Really?" Gran frowned at him as she set a cup of coffee down in front of Arianne.

"What? It's a legitimate question." Pa took another sip of his coffee and reached for some toast.

"It is, Gran," Arianne said.

Gran looked chagrined.

"It's no use us tiptoeing around on eggshells." Arianne took a bite of her toast. "Either I face the reality of my new condition and grasp new opportunities, or I will sit wrapped in cotton wool and drowning in self-pity."

"I'm sorry," Gran said. "Thanks for being open and honest."

"Anyway, today is just an introduction. The country club has a pool that some of the older members use for aqua aerobics. The woman I spoke to said they had accommodated rehabilitation therapy before, though they're not specifically trained."

"What did your physiotherapist say?" Gran sat down at the table.

"He printed the program out and sent it to the personal trainer at the gym. I have a copy as well."

"Is it safe?" Pa asked.

"What could possibly go wrong?" Arianne took a sip of her coffee and smiled at them. "It can't get any worse."

Gran looked horrified, and Pa just stared at her.

"I'm joking," she said. "I've done most of these exercises before. Even if they don't know what they're doing, I can coach them on how to assist."

There were a few tense moments while they ate breakfast.

"Look, guys." Arianne broke the silence. "I have to joke and look at the bright side. I can't be morbid about this."

"You're right," Gran said. "We're just trying to get our heads around it."

"Thanks." Arianne smiled at them both. "The reason I came here was because Mom and Dad couldn't get their heads around it, and they were smothering me."

"And your boyfriend?"

"Gavin?" Arianne was surprised they'd brought him up and felt the shard of rejection as she recalled what he'd done.

"I assume you've broken it off with him," Gran said.

"It took you a while to bring him up, but yeah," Arianne said. "He's long gone." She tried to keep the bitterness from her tone, though it was coating every memory she had of her former boyfriend.

"Perhaps you'll find someone new here in Trinity Lakes." Pa didn't seem to sense that there was an issue in discussing Gavin —or the possibilities of her love life. Like Lucy's brother, Matt, who could scarcely look at her. Sure, finding a new relationship was going to be easy—not. Arianne ruthlessly pushed thoughts about Gavin and any possible relationship to the back of her mind. She was a person with a disability now, and finding someone who could see past that had severely lowered her chances. Best to focus on learning to embrace life as best she could, despite her limitations.

———

"Be careful, darlin'." Pa set Arianne in her chair outside the country club. "I am happy to come in with you, if you want."

"Thanks, Pa. I know you want to help, but I need to build confidence and independence, and this is relatively low risk. Just help me up the incline. The personal trainer already knows I'm coming, so it should be good."

Arianne wished she could be free to wheel everywhere. Her lack of strength on her right side was one of the reasons she was here. For the time being, she needed to be thankful for her grandfather. Arianne smiled and squeezed his hand before he took hold of the wheelchair and guided her up the access ramp of the two-story building.

He leaned down and pecked her on the cheek. "Text me when you've finished, and I'll swing by and pick you up."

"Thanks, Pa." Arianne waved as he left.

Wow. This was some place. There were tennis courts and the large golf course she'd seen as they'd driven into the parking lot. At least the club had excellent access for wheelchairs—a smooth carpark and a proper access ramp. A new day. A new opportunity. The potential for new friends. She took a deep breath and approached the sliding door leading to the main reception area.

Nice.

The lobby was classy. The light-oak reception desk with silver metal wrap around panels stood in front of a wall with the name Trinity Lakes Country Club in a standout font. She didn't need to report there because the signs were clear. Administration and offices off to the right. Restaurant and golf-pro shop straight ahead and a sign that indicated the gym was on the lower level. Elevators with buttons at wheelchair level. Hooray. What a beautiful place, with so many possibilities.

Then it hit her. She wasn't going to be playing tennis or golf anytime soon, and the memory of her newly acquired condition ripped at the grief that lay raw, just below the surface. Arianne punched the button to the elevator, blinking back the tears that stung her eyes. Self-pity lay at her door, ready to pounce at any moment.

By the time the elevator door opened into the lobby of the gym, she'd managed to rein in her emotions and pasted on a smile. New possibilities. New friendships. Strengthening her body and her soul—until the personal trainer behind the desk looked her way and all her hopes sank like a stone. Lucy's brother. Of all the people in the world ... why him?

———

OF ALL THE people in the world ... why her? Though he'd shrugged off the idea, it seemed she really was Adam's client. His stomach knotted. How on earth was he supposed to train her? She obviously couldn't walk.

"Matt! What are you doing?" Jeannette spoke in a whispered warning tone and walked straight past him.

"Hi." Jeannette's tone was bright and friendly as she approached the Rayne's granddaughter.

What was her name? He wished his memory worked better these days, but he'd felt like he was in a mental fog since the conversation about Jane.

"Welcome to Trinity Lakes and welcome to our country club. Adam Lancaster has sent us your program, so we're all set to begin. Right, Matt?" Jeanette didn't look back in his direction, but he could hear that underlying rebuke in her tone.

Just like Lucy. Why were they so self-righteous? This working with the disabled wasn't easy when he'd had no experience whatsoever. He couldn't do this. He should've begged off straight away when Adam had mentioned his client was this girl.

Jeannette picked up the clipboard with the program on it from the reception desk. She looked it over, then handed it to him.

"Arianne, my name's Jeanette. I'm the coordinator here. This is Matt Kennedy. He'll be working with you as you do your upper body and shoulder-strengthening exercises. I'll help you with the hydrotherapy exercises if you don't mind me swapping him out. I've done this before with another client."

"That would be great. Thank you." She looked relieved. That

made two of them. He still had to do the weights and resistance training with her, unless he could get out of that as well.

"Let's start in the pool today, if that's okay with you. We have an aqua aerobics class in an hour, so it's better to use the pool now, while it's not busy. Okay?" Jeanette kept talking as if it was the most natural thing in the world. Matthew didn't know if he could do it. He felt so uncomfortable.

"The changing rooms are over there. Do you need any help?"

"Unfortunately, I still do at this stage. Not for much longer, hopefully. Is there a locker for my bag?"

Jeanette retrieved a key from behind the desk and handed it to Arianne. "The lockers are inside the changing rooms. I'll meet you there in a few minutes."

Arianne wheeled away and into the changing rooms. The moment she disappeared, Jeanette turned on him. "What is the matter with you?"

"What?"

"This is a new client. First, you ignore her as she comes in, then you've been looking at her as if she's an alien."

"I'm not trained to deal with this sort of thing." Already he could feel this had shadows of Mr. Searle's lambasting, which underscored his point.

"What sort of thing?" Jeanette wasn't going to let him off the hook.

"You know ..." Matthew waved his hand up and down, indicating waist to toe.

"I don't know. What is your problem?"

"She's ... you know... disabled."

"Good heavens, Matt. If I'd known you were so ableist, I wouldn't have employed you."

"Ableist? What are you talking about?"

"We'll talk about this later." Jeannette left him at reception and disappeared into the changing rooms, leaving Matthew bewildered.

31

When Jeannette and Arianne emerged from the women's locker room Arianne wore full length yoga pants and a sleeveless training top. Her left arm was ripped with great muscle condition, and it was obvious which shoulder had been injured. He'd seen shoulder injuries improve after rehabilitation before, but she was still in a wheelchair. How was Jeanette going to manage getting her into the pool? They disappeared into the pool area and Matthew moved into the weight room. There were two clients already at work there, both of whom preferred to work independently.

Matthew looked over the program Adam had sent through. He was familiar with all the exercises, but how on earth was he to get her to move from one piece of training equipment to the other? He would ask Jeannette to take her on. This was too hard for him.

The bell rang at reception. Matthew went to answer, as Jeannette was working with Arianne.

"Hi." A tall, young woman with strawberry-blond hair turned and beamed a million-kilowatt smile in his direction.

"Hello." Matthew found himself smiling as he approached. Here was a client he could work with, with no traumatic childhood memories making him want to run and hide.

"I'd like to sign up for a membership."

"Absolutely." Matthew hurried over to the desk and retrieved the tablet. He opened the page that gave the introductory information and all the disclaimers.

"If you would like to take a seat and read through the first two pages, you'll find the sign-up forms following. You can fill them in and give them back to me. I'll be happy to walk you through various programs." Even as he went through the spiel, he paused a millisecond. She was holding up her mobile phone on a selfie stick and turned around, moving next to him so that they were both in the camera frame. It took extra willpower to continue and resist the frown threatening to form.

When he handed the tablet to her, she stepped away, and pushed the telescope stick in with a snap. "I hope you don't mind if I record my experiences for my social media fans."

What was he supposed to say? Perhaps this would be good exposure for the country club.

"Do you have a lot of followers?" he asked.

"Followers? Are you kidding?" She batted her false eyelashes in his direction as if she were in shock. "Do you mean to say you don't know who I am?"

Matthew's mouth went dry. She was gorgeous enough to be a model or movie star, but her face wasn't familiar. How embarrassing.

"Heidi's World?"

Matthew felt like an idiot, blinking his eyes, but nothing came to mind.

"Sorry. I'm not on social media much."

A handful of fake decorated nails, complete with little diamonds in a heart shape, clapped over her mouth. "Get out. You haven't heard of me?"

"I have now." He threw his best grin in her direction. Did he look as big a fool as he felt?

"Well, I hope you start following me. I have over three million subscribers."

He struggled to swallow. The moisture from his mouth had failed to return.

"Don't worry, babes. You'll catch on." She kissed him on the cheek and took the tablet.

What was that crazy cyclone of adrenaline that almost knocked him over? Babes? Heidi sat on the leather sofa, her white sneakers set together in a neat toe-pointed pose as she began to tap her manicured nails on the screen. If it wasn't for the phone ringing, he would have remained frozen in that mesmerized state like an open-mouthed idiot.

BEING in the water brought so much support for her lower limbs. Arianne had done this before at the rehab center near her parents' home, resting on her back, a floating device around her neck and a pool noodle beneath her knees. Using the water weights to do the arm, shoulder and abdominal core exercises felt good. She could feel the muscles exercising and strength building—in her upper body. Her legs floated uselessly in the warm water. She strained to detect any sensation. The warm water was magnificent on her skin in the areas where the nerves still sent messages.

"You're doing great." Jeanette was in the water behind her, handing the different weights to her, and coaching her along in the various exercises. "You've obviously done this before."

"Yeah. As soon as my injury stabilized, they were encouraging various exercises."

"How long have you been in rehab?"

There was no need to pause to calculate. Arianne was well aware of the date and exactly how many months, weeks, and days it had been since her life had been tipped upside down. But she did pause before eventually answering. "It will be six months next week."

Arianne sensed Jeanette wanted to ask more, but her sensitivity restrained her. Was she ready to trust this woman she'd met only this morning?

"I had a car accident." Arianne blurted it out, chasing away any doubt.

"Do you want to talk about it?" Jeannette asked, before showing Arianne a different rotation of exercises to do.

Did she want to talk about it? There were so many things about the accident and the way Gavin had reacted that were buried beneath the other trauma of adjusting to life without walking. The counselor at the rehab center hadn't even gotten close, and whenever her mother had brought the subject up, Arianne had shut it down. She hadn't been ready to face it.

Jeanette did not pry further. What a wise and sensitive woman.

"My boyfriend was driving. He was way over the speed limit and I asked him to slow down, but he just laughed and went faster." Arianne paused as she remembered that horrible night.

"I'm sorry," Jeannette said. "You don't have to tell me if it's uncomfortable."

"He lost control on a bend in the road, and I can't remember much after that. They told me the car hit a tree and that I was lucky to come out alive."

There was silence from behind. Jeanette could have offered platitudes. Arianne had heard plenty of those in the last few months.

"I'm sorry, Jeannette. This must be awkward for you."

"I confess, I don't know what's the right thing to say."

Arianne gave a short laugh. "I don't think there is a right thing to say. But thank you for listening. I haven't talked about it with anyone since the accident."

"How did your boyfriend fare in the accident?"

"He walked away with a few stitches and a minor concussion."

"That must have been ..." Jeanette broke off from what she was going to say.

"Yeah. It might have been a relief that he wasn't badly injured or killed, but by the time I'd gained consciousness, they'd worked out I was probably never going to walk again, and I found it difficult to think about anybody but myself. Does that sound selfish?"

"It sounds understandable."

"Well, he thought it was selfish. And he also thought it was best if we broke up, because he didn't want to wait around to see if I was ever going to get better."

As the words came out, a surge of bitterness felt like bile in her mouth, followed quickly by a sense of shame. She wasn't supposed to be full of anger and resentment. She was supposed to have forgiven Gavin—but she hadn't. He'd caused the accident that had destroyed her life, then he'd walked away. How was that fair? *God, that isn't fair.*

"Are you all right?" Jeannette swam in closer and took the weights from Arianne's hands. "I'm sorry, Ari. That must be painful for you."

Arianne used her arms to turn over and swim to the edge of the pool. Painful was an understatement. She was angry and bitter and full of shame and regret, and she didn't know what on earth she was supposed to do with it.

"Shall we complete this session, or would you prefer to finish up?" Jeanette put the weights on the side of the pool.

"I can't pack it in every time I have a surge of emotion from the past. Otherwise I'll just sit home and do nothing. Can we do the leg exercises? Do you mind?"

"I don't mind. You'll have to tell me if I'm doing them right."

Arianne smiled at the trainer. "I'm glad you're helping with this. I'm afraid your other personal trainer would struggle."

Jeannette gave a short laugh. "I'm sorry about Matt. I don't know what got into him. I've never seen him be so rude to a client."

"Don't worry about it. I get that from time to time."

"Get what?"

"People who can't cope with someone who's living with a disability. They just want to pretend we don't exist."

"That can't be right. Surely not."

"You might be right. I'm probably overreacting."

"Well, if you've met behavior like we saw with Matt this morning, then it's not overreacting. I felt like giving him a swift kick to snap him out of it."

Arianne laughed. "I would like to see you try. That would make me feel a whole lot better."

———

HEIDI GLASSEN WAS like a whirlwind of personality who commanded attention. No wonder she had millions of social media followers. Matthew looked her up while she was in the locker rooms and saw that she was a well-known influencer, with loads of sponsors. By the look of her, it appeared she was sponsored by a makeup company, and possibly a Botox company. It was glamor and glitz—fake on so many levels—but attractive and he was drawn to the circle of light and excitement surrounding her.

And she seemed to like him.

"So Matthew, I'd like to introduce you to my followers." This was not a request for permission, as she already had her phone on a stick angled in his direction. "Tell everyone what you hope to achieve with my training program."

He could see his profile on her screen. He should sharpen up his smile.

"With these guns, I've got high hopes of getting some well-toned muscles." Without giving him time to answer, she squeezed his arm as she focused the phone in that direction. Matthew felt color climb in his cheeks.

He stepped a few inches away and scrambled to assemble some sensible thoughts, but she'd moved on.

"Stay tuned, peeps. I've got some work to do, getting all hot and sweaty." She blew a kiss toward her phone and switched it off.

"You're gorgeous, Matthew. My followers will eat you up."

Matthew's mouth had gone dry again. Heidi was so fast-paced, he had a job to keep up with her. He had a moment of euphoria at the compliment—gorgeous, she'd said. But then a sensible thought, a thought that sounded remarkably like his sister, hit him in the back of the head. *You're an idiot. She's just using you. Objectifying you. Get a grip and be a professional.*

Matthew had a beginner's program loaded on his tablet, so he ushered Heidi towards the weights room. How much work could he get done before she went live again? Crazy times.

Twenty minutes later, he knew. This whole excursion to the gym, and engaging a personal trainer, was about online content. And she wasn't shy about the innuendo cast in his direction. He was fit and had the benefit of regular gym workouts, but apparently, he was handsome as well. Who knew? Was he flattered? Well, yeah. It was kind of exciting, and a bit disturbing at the same time. He wasn't sure she would have benefited much from the session, as she'd spent a lot of time reengaging her followers, and not nearly enough time rotating through the exercises.

"Matt? Can I speak to you for a moment, please?" Jeanette came from the direction of the changing rooms and put her clipboard in the tray at reception, ready to be filed.

"Sure." There was a cold feeling of chagrin swirling in the pit of his stomach. "I just signed up a new client." It would be best to lead with something positive, as he had the feeling he was about to be lectured.

"Yes. I saw." Jeanette's lips were rolled in a tight line of disapproval.

"She's a social media influencer. She's got millions of followers and has named our gym as a place to come." Why was he babbling?

"Right." She didn't sound impressed.

"How did you go with the disabled girl?"

Just as he said it, the woman in question rolled out from the locker room. Her wet dark brown hair had been brushed back into a knot and left her face clear of dangling strands. She looked fresh. Had she heard him? She had a pleasant smile on her face, but it didn't quite reach her sparking dark eyes. She had heard him. She was not happy. Guilt rushed up and flushed his face.

"Arianne and I have decided it would be best if I did all her training." Jeannette's tone held an underlying rebuke.

"Sure. Right. That will probably be best." Matthew cast a quick smile in Arianne's direction. Arianne. He needed to remember her name.

Jeannette turned to the girl in the wheelchair. "I'll book you for tomorrow morning, and we can do an extended session— half in the pool and half in the gym. I'm excited to work with you."

"Thanks, Jeannette." Arianne smiled warmly at Jeannette, a genuine smile that reached her eyes. Huh? "I've sent a text to Pa, so I'll go outside and wait for him in the parking lot."

"Do you need any help?" Jeannette asked.

"No. I'm fine. Pa won't take long to get here. Thanks again for the session. I really enjoyed it." She flexed her arm muscles and directed her chair to the elevators.

Matthew watched, intrigued. Once that shoulder was fully rehabilitated, she would be strong. If he hadn't missed his guess, she was annoyed with him. Well, it didn't matter. It was best if Jeannette took her on. She obviously had the gift to work with all the difficulties.

As the girl disappeared into the elevator, Matthew turned, ready to receive the lecture.

"I'm not finished with you yet," Jeannette said, "but you'd better sign out your other 'new client'." She used air quotes. Did she think that Heidi wasn't a real client? Well, whatever.

At that moment, Heidi emerged from the changing rooms. She had a new layer of makeup, and her hair was styled—as if she'd used some kind of hot tongs or something. It certainly was not a fresh-from-a-workout look. What did she have in her sports bag?

"Thanks for choosing us to help with your fitness goals."

Matthew met her before she could go to the elevators. "How many times a week do you think you'd like to come in? I can book regular sessions if you'd like."

"You're so cute, babes." She kissed him on the cheek. "And so patient. I couldn't believe you let disabled people into your pool. What if she'd drowned?"

Matthew frowned. Was that what he sounded like when talking about the girl? It didn't sound nice in his ears.

"Jeannette is competent. She would have taken care of her and not let anything happen."

"Still. It's kind of gloopy."

Gloopy? "Sorry?" Matthew wasn't really sorry. An unsettled feeling swirled in his stomach.

"Never mind, babes. So long as she's not here tomorrow when I'm filming."

"She might be. I think Jeanette has booked her four times a week."

"Ugh. That's awkward. Let me see her times so I can avoid them. It's not the kind of image I want to present to my followers."

Seriously? Matthew felt agitated but checked the schedule anyway. After they'd negotiated the times in the week that Heidi intended to come in and train, Matthew walked her to the door.

"I'll see you tomorrow then."

"I'll be ready anticipating all kinds of deliciousness." She pressed her manicured fingertips to her lips and blew him yet another kiss. She was something else.

CHAPTER FOUR

The next morning, Jeanette shoved a brochure into Matthew's hand after he'd stowed his sports bag in the cupboard behind the reception desk.

"Thanks. What's this?"

"Our policy on inclusion. Read it and then let's review yesterday's debacle and discuss, all right?"

"Inclusion?"

"Please, Matthew Kennedy. You must understand our policy for inclusion—though after yesterday's performance, I'm beginning to wonder."

"Are you talking about ..." What was the Rayne girl's name? Think. Think. "Arrabel?"

"My case in point. You need to sharpen up, young man, or you might find yourself with a write-up if that behavior from yesterday continues."

She was truly upset about this. He didn't have so many job options that he was fool enough to disrespect his boss. "I'm sorry, Jeanette. Perhaps I'm not as well-versed in inclusion as I should be."

"You don't say."

"I'll read the policy, but would you mind pointing out the main issues for me to think about?"

"At least you're big enough to realize you've made a mistake, because if you'd resisted me on this, I would seriously have to consider your future here."

Matthew nodded, searching for moisture in his mouth. She was really upset and he guessed it had to do with ... Arrabel? ... Arianne. Yes, that's it. Her name was Arianne.

Jeanette held out her hand for the brochure, which he sheepishly handed back to her. She opened to the contents page and jabbed her finger at the first heading.

"Access."

"We have disabled parking spaces." Matthew hadn't paid particular attention before, but now that Jeanette was on her crusade, he felt pleased that he knew this. "And there are elevators so she can get down to our level."

Why was Jeanette rolling her eyes—and a huff as well?

"It's more than just access parking and elevators, Matt. This is about our training environment being welcoming for all people, no matter age, ability, fitness, or any other criteria we could name."

"Right." His tone showed the uncertainty he felt.

"And a welcoming environment should foster an atmosphere that shows the staff have a friendly, can-do attitude, even when there are people who present with unexpected challenges."

Matthew's dry mouth persisted. He wasn't confident or competent or comfortable with this.

"Do you have any idea how awful you were yesterday?" Jeanette held him in a first-class glare.

He wanted to cite the incident with Mr. Searle that had been followed up by a stern lecture from his parents. "I'm not confident ..."

"Confident? Confident?" Matthew hadn't seen Jeanette so worked up about something before, and, too late, the revelation of his wrongdoing was jumping out to accuse him. "This is not about confidence, Matt. This is about professional development. If you've not worked with an aged client or a client with disability before, that has nothing to do with your welcoming attitude. I'll bet you haven't trained a social influencer before, and yet you managed to be polite and friendly."

"That is slightly different."

"Of course it's different. But that's not the point. I understand you may never have had the opportunity to assist someone with mobility challenges, so now you have the opportunity, it's time for you to do some professional development and learn."

Several objections floated around in his mind, each one quickly shot down by Jeanette's firm "no argument" demeanor.

"At the moment, you could easily be accused of being ableist …"

Ableist? He'd only heard the term used for the first time this week and hadn't known such a condition existed. But he wasn't being asked to speak.

"And given we have older clients, if you carry on like you did yesterday towards them, you'll be fitted with an ageist label as well."

This kept getting better and better. He wouldn't have considered himself the sort of person who could have been accused of anything—yet now it was being held up like a mirror in his face, he had to concede. There was such an attitude. And apparently, he had it.

"And given you call yourself a Christian …"

Oh no. She was going there as well.

"… I would have thought inclusion would have been top of your list.

Jeanette didn't subscribe to religion as far as he knew, but, as with all small towns, she knew his faith status. Right at this moment, things looked ugly. Of course she was right. Even he'd noticed Heidi's rude—ableist—comments. The term was new in his vocabulary, but he could see now what it was, and felt a rush of shame to realize he'd engaged in the same sort of hurtful behavior. This was awful. And yet, shame or no shame, the idea he might have to help Arianne remained overwhelming.

"There are several courses you can do to expand your training." Jeanette flicked the brochure with the back of her fingers. "I'll help you find one if you need it, but I do not want to see a repeat of yesterday's performance. Ever. Understand?"

"You're right. I'm sorry."

"Good." Jeanette passed the brochure back to him. "You can find some courses in this brochure. Let me know how you go with them."

———

"ALL SET?" Pa bent to lift Arianne up and guide her into his SUV. She nodded and took the ride.

"I can't wait until I can do this transfer myself." Arianne clicked her seat belt into place.

"I'm sure I can't figure out how you'll manage to do this yourself. I don't want to sound like a negative Nancy, but…" Pa shrugged his shoulders before putting the key into the ignition.

"I've seen it done, and I've enrolled in a special rehabilitation class in Walla Walla in a couple of months to focus specifically on transferring. I'm hoping my gym sessions will have been enough to have strengthened my right shoulder by then."

"But how is it done? I can't imagine it." Pa kept his eyes on the road as they travelled the miles to the Trinity Lakes Country Club.

"With a slide board. I have one, but I haven't used it yet. It's taken longer than I'd hoped to regain strength in my shoulder, so I couldn't get any practice before I left hospital."

"So you, what, set the board on your chair? How do you fit it in the truck?"

Arianne laughed and shook her head. "I couldn't get into a truck with it. The height difference from the seat of the chair to the front seat of the truck is way too high."

"What about Gran's SUV? That's high as well."

"It is. I know. I'm kind of hoping I'll be able to buy a smaller sedan or hatchback. If you park the car in a level place with plenty of room for the wheelchair, the board will be almost level."

"You want to buy a car? Do you think you'll ever be able to drive?"

"I haven't looked into it thoroughly yet, but I understand there are modifications that can be made so the gas and brake are operated by hand."

"You're not afraid?"

"Pa!" She turned a frown on her grandfather. "Of course I'm afraid. But I don't have anything else to pursue in life at the moment, so I may as well do everything I can to regain mobility and independence. Hence why we're going to the gym so much."

"Right. I'm sorry, darlin'. Let me help you as much as I can."

"Thanks, Pa. I'm glad you're here, able, and willing. You're a Godsend."

"Speaking of a Godsend," Pa continued, "There's a healing evangelist scheduled to come through Trinity Lakes later next month."

It was an innocent comment, but the words sent a stab of fear through Arianne's heart.

"Do you think you'd like to go for prayer?"

Arianne sucked in a deep breath. Faith. Healing. Miracles. These words were all part of her pre-accident vernacular. She'd seen healing evangelists before. Had invited friends to attend rallies. Had offered to pray for friends who needed a miracle.

She believed in God's power to heal. Would never deny it. And yet ...

"You still have faith, right, darlin'?"

"Yes, Pa. I still have faith." But there was more to it than faith. It was too convoluted in her mind for her to be able to articulate clearly what she felt.

"I'll look into the service times and see if we can all go as a family."

Arianne didn't answer. The last thing she wanted to do was go to a healing meeting. They'd prayed for her at the hospital, and she'd lived. She hadn't thanked God for that at the time, as the loss of mobility crowded in to squash any gratitude she might have felt.

But it wasn't that so much as the opinions of several people she'd met who worked in advocacy for people with disabilities. All had experienced loss—some more than her—and had lived with those losses for many years. Some had spoken to her about seeing herself as a whole person as she was, that she was as valuable as anyone without a disability. It was true. It had to be true—though there were plenty of times she cried at night, asking God why he'd allowed the accident to happen. There had been other times when she'd questioned her value. She was a burden. At the moment, at least, she was a burden to her grandparents, despite their protests that it was a privilege for them to have her stay with them.

Pa parked his truck in front of the country club. Arianne had been quiet for the last five minutes, still trying to confront the question of healing, but Pa didn't seem to have noticed. He got out and unloaded her wheelchair from the back of the vehicle, wheeling it around to her open passenger door.

"If you like, I'll keep my eye out for a good small car." Pa held out his arms to help her from the front seat. "If you don't mind, I'll do some research on these newfangled hand controls. Okay with you?"

Arianne lifted her stubborn useless legs onto the footrests one at a time. "Given I know very little about cars, I'd be grateful if you would. Small steps."

"Small steps." Pa kissed her cheek and wheeled her toward the ramp. Once she'd made the level surface, he left her to make her own way toward the front door. He'd adjusted quickly to letting her do as much as she was able, but how was this conversation about God's healing power going to go? It would happen one day soon. She couldn't keep putting it off, but even she didn't know what the answer was. What happened if God's answer was "no"?

Arianne wheeled straight over to the elevator and hit the button for the basement gym. Time to brace herself to face Mr. Warm and Wonderful. Anxiety screwed a ball in her stomach. It was hard enough being ignored by anyone, but when it was a cute, buff guy, and his rejection was blatant, it made her feel ugly—unattractive, worthless, without value.

But she refused to let his attitude keep her from her goal—muscle strength and perhaps developing some new neural pathways that would help her stand upright. And move? Perhaps that was too much to hope for.

As the elevator door opened, she was greeted by the man himself. She braced, anticipating yesterday's pretend-she-wasn't-there blank stare, but instead he almost launched himself at her.

"Good morning, Arianne."

What was that in his tone? "Good morning." She found her tone tilting up as a question. Did it sound like she was suspicious? She was suspicious.

"How are you feeling today?"

Aah. Now she recognized the tone. It was pity. Or was it patronizing? Either way, it wasn't great.

"I'm well, thank you, Matthew. How are you feeling today?"

She saw a shade of red creep into his face. Why? Was he

sorry for yesterday, or did he realize that today wasn't much better?

"Do you need help getting ready for your session?"

It was pity. Was that better than ignoring her? That was a question worth debating. He was a bit of a Neanderthal, really.

"I'm fine, thanks. Is Jeanette here?" Arianne looked around, hoping the other trainer would materialize.

"She's with some other clients right now. She asked me to get you set up in the weights room. She'll be with you in a few minutes."

"Right. I'll just go and stow my bag."

"Do you need me to do it for you?"

Good grief. This guy was so clueless. It was all she could do not to shake her head.

"That's very kind, but there are many things I am still capable of. Stowing my bag is one of them." She wheeled toward the locker room, then had a moment of regret. Her words and tone were a bit reactive, bordering on rude. Should she be sorry and put up with this condescension? It wasn't her nature to be so sensitive and rude. Bother her personal values. Matthew Kennedy was a clueless clown, but it was probably because he was ignorant. Should she cut him some slack? She blew out a small sniff of disgust. *All right, God. If you want me to be kind, I will be kind.*

———

Wow! What had he done wrong this time? He'd said "good morning" in a friendly way. He'd offered to help her with whatever she needed. Why had she snapped his head off? It was like Mr. Searle all over again. There was no getting it right. He was glad Jeanette was otherwise occupied with a small group of older women doing water aerobics. He'd tried.

He went to the computer, opened the online course he'd

enrolled in, and reviewed the introductory lesson. Friendly, kind, welcoming. He'd done that. This was going to be harder than he'd thought. Both Lucy and Jeanette had challenged his attitude, and if he hadn't seen Heidi in action, he might not have known what they were talking about. But something had struck him as inherently wrong the way Heidi had talked about Arianne. That didn't mean he was any the wiser as to where he'd gone wrong this morning.

God, I could use some of your wisdom.

When Arianne emerged from the locker room, she looked ready. Focused. Stern?

"Listen, Matthew." She guided her wheelchair over to him. "I realize this might be new for you, and perhaps you haven't thought it through, but heads up—I'm not a child, and I hate pity. There are some things I can do perfectly well, and others I'm working on improving. And other things I may never be able to do again, but I'm a normal human being ..." She paused, as if she had more to say, but had thought better of it. Well, that was good, because he was still trying to process the first sentence.

"I'm sorry. I've been less than helpful," he said. "You're right —I don't know what I'm doing. I appreciate your frankness."

"Good. Well, I'm sorry for my outburst before. Could we start over?" She held her hand out for him to shake.

Would he hurt her? Idiot. She wouldn't offer to shake hands if it would hurt her. He carefully took her hand and shook gently. "Nice to meet you. Let me know if there is anything else I can do to help you."

"Thank you." She smiled, and something shifted inside Matthew. She was just like any other client. Except for the wheelchair thing.

"So we're starting in the weights room?" Arianne turned her chair in that direction. "I assume you have a copy of the program."

Matthew turned back and grabbed the clipboard from the desk. He would get her started. If only he could figure out how to get her from the chair to the bench of the shoulder press machine.

"Ah. Help me out, Arianne. I'd like you to start with shoulder presses, but ..." He waved his hand between the wheelchair and the bench seat.

"How do I transfer?" She gave him a smile.

He nodded.

"One day, I hope to be able to do it myself. Today, you get to lift me across. Do you think you can manage?"

A shaft of cold panic sliced through his stomach. This was soooo outside his comfort zone. What would happen if he tried to lift her? Would he hurt her?

"Relax." Arianne's steady voice cut through his fearful fog. "I'll talk you through. You can't go far wrong."

Far wrong? Good gravy. He didn't want to touch her for fear of going wrong at all.

Arianne wheeled her chair up to the shoulder press bench and parked at a forty-five degree angle, facing forward, then set her brakes. She deftly disconnected a side piece that slid out of the chair, and she handed it to him.

"Can you put this somewhere we won't forget it."

Matthew took the steel piece and slid it under the bench.

"Now, take hold of my legs, beneath my knees." Arianne's voice was commanding and confident, the complete opposite of what he felt. Take hold of her legs. Was she crazy?

"Come on, Matthew. You can do this."

"Easy for you to say."

"But not easy for me to do. I need you to help me, if you will try."

A wave of shame hit him. He'd been insensitive again, but she'd called him on it. So, take hold of her legs. Don't think about it. Don't think about it.

"Like this." Arianne leaned forward and grabbed her legs beneath her knees. This was so awkward, but he had to learn.

Tentatively and carefully, he put his hands beneath her knees as she'd requested.

"Now, pull my legs forward so my butt slides to the front of the chair—don't pull too hard, or I'll end up on the ground."

Matthew swallowed. She sounded like she was laughing at him. This was honestly the craziest thing he'd ever done—which might have been an exaggeration, but he didn't have time to review.

"Just pull carefully, Matthew. You can do it."

He pulled. She slid forward.

"Woah. Stop. That's enough. Now, quickly, put your arms under my arms and around behind my back, and don't forget to bend your legs so you don't hurt your back."

So many instructions. He leaned forward, afraid she was going to fall out of the chair, and slid his arms beneath her arms and around behind her back.

"Now, using your leg and core muscles, lift and swing me onto the bench."

He did as commanded and lifted. She wasn't that heavy. Not heavy at all really, and he soon had her seated, a little crooked, on the shoulder press bench.

"Now let go."

Too late, he realized he still had his arms around her, his face next to hers. With embarrassment burning his cheeks he drew back, but still held her shoulders.

"I'm not going to topple over, Matthew. It's okay. I can take it from here."

"Are you sure?"

She gave him a potent narrow-eyed look.

"Right. Of course you're sure. You don't want to be babied."

Using her hands, she bent and lifted her left leg up onto the bench and then placed it on the other side so that she now straddled the bench. Matthew hovered in case he needed to help her, but she seemed perfectly balanced as she used her arms to shuffle and get into position.

"Right. So what weight do you suggest I start at?"

The whole process happened so quickly Matthew was dizzy trying to piece together all the steps. The one that kept flashing in his mind was the lift—well, not the lift—the arms around her, his face next to hers. That was a part of the process that felt wrong. No, it felt right, but it was wrong. Wasn't it? How confusing was this?

"You've already started." Jeannette's voice startled him as she approached from behind. "Bravo, Matt. I assume you did the lifting."

Still flustered, he just nodded his head.

"Great work. I can take it from here. You go and sort out those personal training programs for the two new clients."

Right.

"See ya, Matthew."

Matthew spun back around. He'd forgotten to say goodbye. When was he going to get this? Arianne was an ordinary person. "Right. Thanks. I'll catch you later."

Would he? Catch her later? He'd faced and overcome one fear, but that didn't mean he was bursting to be in charge again. It was best if Jeannette was her trainer. She was less likely to be clunky and insensitive.

CHAPTER FIVE

Heidi Glasson arrived on time in a whirl of glitter and strong-smelling perfume. She batted her false eyelashes at Matthew and kissed him on the cheek.

"Hi, babes."

It was inappropriate, but his ego reveled in the attention.

"Do you mind?" Heidi had her phone mounted on a selfie-stick and her finger hovered over the record button. The question was obviously rhetorical because she didn't wait for an answer before pressing record, putting her arm around his waist and her head as close to his as she could, given their difference in height.

"So here I am. Day two, peeps, with the gorgeous Matthew." She beamed a smile up in his direction. "What have you got in store for me today, Matthew?"

He was so not a media person. His mouth had gone dry again, and even though he'd already reviewed her notes in preparation, all sensible thought deserted him.

"That's what I love about you." She kissed him again, this time for Heidi's World to see on live stream. "It appears we might need a quiet moment together before we can get an answer for you." She pressed fingertips to her lips and blew a kiss to cyber world. "Stand by. I'll see you in a few."

What was with him today? First Arianne, now Heidi. Both women had his head in a whirl, and it was so unprofessional. He picked up the clipboard with the planned exercise rotations written out and directed Heidi towards the Pilates space. Stretching first.

"I saw the wheelchair girl leaving as I came in. Did you get stuck with her, or did you manage to wiggle out of it?" Heidi directed a smile his way.

"Jeannette is in charge of her training—"

"I'll bet you're glad about that. No avoiding her altogether though, I suppose?"

What could he say? It was as if Heidi had read his thoughts—yesterday's thoughts, the thoughts he'd had before Jeannette had delivered her lecture.

"Just be thankful you don't have to see her every day."

Should he say something? Lucy would have exploded all over the ceiling by this point. And Jeannette would have offered a friendly speech on kindness and inclusion. But it was as if Heidi had picked him on her team and drawn him into her inner circle, and he wasn't confident enough to risk offending her, so he kept his mouth shut, and offered a weak smile.

By the time Heidi had moved her online audience into the locker room, he had managed to get a few exercises going, but not without him being filmed and fawned over. Did he like it? Not really, if he was being honest. Heidi didn't censor any of her comments or show any sensitivity to how he might feel being objectified. But he didn't say anything. His sisters, mother, and Jeannette would boil him in rubbing liniment if he ever made those kinds of comments about a woman. He wouldn't anyway. He hated it when other guys did it. But what about when a girl did it to him—and on social media? Heidi had shown him some of the emojis and responses from her fans. It wasn't flattering—not when it was a mass media response from who knows what sorts of women.

"Say, Matthew?" Heidi emerged from the locker rooms, a picture-perfect model, and walked over to him. "I should say thank you for appearing in my live streams."

Not that she'd asked his permission. But it was too late now.

"You should see the online activity. My followers are eating it up."

Matthew rolled his lips into a thin line. He didn't really know what to say, because telling her to tone it down—or better yet, cut it out—didn't seem to be an option.

"I'm getting the vibe that you're not really comfortable being an online star." For the first time since he'd met her, she seemed sensitive to him, focused on something other than herself. It was an attractive look on her. "Are you okay?" she asked.

"It's a bit over the top for my tastes."

"I got that, but you're so gorgeous when you're flustered. Please say you'll keep going. My followers love you."

Matthew chased the many thoughts that ran through his mind, trying to catch one that would make sense if he said it out loud.

"Please." Heidi's tone was soft and pleading, and her large eyes were deep pools of gathering moisture. She wasn't going to cry, surely. But the eyes appealed to his heart.

"Would it be okay if you dialed down the innuendo a bit?"

What was that flash in her eyes? Anger? Chagrin? Repentance? It was something, but only for a split second. He hoped it was a display of feeling sorry.

"I didn't realize you were sensitive. I'm sorry." She said the words, but her tone didn't match.

"The whole sex object thing doesn't really fit with my religious ideals."

Heidi drew back, like a cobra ready to strike. "What religious ideals?"

"I'm a Christian. I struggle with ..." Should he say it? She already seemed volatile.

"Struggle with what? Don't tell me you're ..."

You're what? This conversation could head in any direction, and none of the options were good from his point of view.

"I struggle to accept the sexualization in our current social climate."

"Why?" She sounded as if she was astounded.

"Because I'm a Christian." Not a great answer but coming up with intelligent answers to sticky questions had never been his strong suit.

"What's that got to do with it? I'm a Christian. I can't see your point."

Matthew stared at her, blinking in confusion. Of all things, he would never have guessed she was a Christian.

"But you don't seem like a Christian." Had that just come out of his mouth? A cold wash of panic swept him from head to toe, and he wished he could snatch his words back.

"What is a Christian supposed to look like? Isn't it supposed to be about the heart?"

"Well, yeah, but ..."

"What is it about me that you don't approve of?"

Wow. Now she was on the offensive. He should have kept his mouth shut.

"That is so like the usual judgmental attitude I've come to expect." Heidi's expression had transformed from the cheerful flirt to one that shot daggers.

"I'm sorry. You're right. True faith in Christ is a heart thing."

"Yes, well. I'm sorry you're all prudish about how you appear. Next time, I'll try to be more careful of your sensitive nature." Heidi shouldered her large expensive-looking bag and dropped her sparkly covered phone inside. It was obvious she was angry with him, but Matthew couldn't think of anything else to say.

"See you tomorrow?" He heard the tinge of desperation in his tone as it hitched up at the end.

"If you can possibly bear having me here." She cast him a glance that would have melted the polar ice caps and flounced to the elevators.

"Nice work, Matt." Jeanette came up behind him. Man. His boss seemed to have a sixth sense when it came to him saying the wrong thing.

"I'm sure she'll be back."

Jeanette raised her eyebrows.

"I just asked if she could tone down the innuendo in her live streams. I don't really feel comfortable with it."

"I suppose that is a workplace issue, though those sorts of complaints usually come from women against men who sexually harass them."

Matthew shrugged. "I think I offended her."

"No kidding."

"I didn't mean to, but I felt I had to say something."

"As it happens, I was going to speak to you about how much time you spend with her. She kind of monopolizes you when she's here. We do have other clients who could use some attention."

Matthew nodded. This would be a useful line to use, if Heidi came back.

———

"I'VE BEEN LOOKING at small cars for you, Ari." Pa spoke as soon as they were on the road. "It depends on what your budget is, but I think we can get one with a high safety rating at a reasonable price."

"Thanks for doing the research. I'm glad you're looking into safety ratings as well." There was still the issue of her finding the confidence to get behind the wheel again. Sure, she hadn't been driving when the accident happened, but she remembered how easily it had happened. One moment they had been driving along at a frightening speed, and the next she was waking up to her world in turmoil having lost three weeks of her life.

"How are your gym sessions going?" Pa didn't pick up on her internal angst.

"My trainer, Jeanette, is really good. She told me today that she's considered doing more study to work in rehabilitation therapy."

"Isn't she trained now?"

"No. She's only done personal training, which is what we're doing, but I've had to coach her on some exercises that I need doing. Particularly with my legs."

"Legs? I thought you couldn't move them."

"I can't. Well, I can occasionally get a couple of toes to move, but on the whole, no."

"Then why are you exercising them?"

"There is a small chance I might be able to get some new neural pathways established, and some more movement."

"So your injury isn't permanent?"

"Some of it is. But it's an incomplete injury, so there is possibility of getting some small movement back."

"Wow. I thought it was final. That you would always be in a wheelchair."

Arianne steeled herself against the fear that stabbed her. "It might be final," she said. "On the other hand, I might be able to stand up again, with the help of walking aids. I really don't know, but I would like to try whatever I can to improve my situation."

"Perhaps with prayer. You never know."

There it was again. Pa, with his optimistic faith. How she

would love to be able to simply embrace it. But something—probably fear, maybe doubt—kept her from reaching out.

"Well, I'm glad you're getting on well with the trainer."

"Yes, between her and my PT sessions, I'm hoping for some improvement."

"Great."

And it was great. She was even glad that she'd pushed Matthew and forced him to engage with her. In the end, he'd responded reasonably well, for someone who had no idea.

"By the way, we're off to midweek Bible study at the Kennedys' house tonight. Would you like to come?"

Arianne glanced over at Pa as he drove.

"I don't know, Pa. I've never met these people, and it might be awkward."

"You met Lucy Kennedy at church, and you said you liked her. She'll probably be there."

Lucy. That meant her brother would be there as well.

"I'm not sure, Pa."

"Well, let me be sure for you. It will be good for you to meet the families around here, and perhaps get to know some of the young people better."

Should she go? Bible study had always been something she enjoyed. And she had liked Lucy. But what if Matthew was there? He was such a difficult person to work out.

"Ari's coming with us to Bible study tonight," he said to Gran as she greeted them in the front hall. They weren't inside the house for ten seconds, and Pa had already accepted the plans as confirmed.

"That's wonderful, Ari. I'm so pleased." Gran kissed her cheek.

"I feel a little awkward." Arianne decided to preempt her begging off.

"Of course you do. That's natural. Once you've been the first time, you'll feel more comfortable next time. The Kennedys are lovely people."

"I met Lucy at church a couple of weeks ago." Arianne wheeled herself into the main living area and her grandparents followed.

"That's right. And you liked her, didn't you?" Gran asked.

"I did, but I'm not eight years old. I can't have you trying to find friends for me."

"Quite right." Gran brought a plate of cookies out and placed them on the coffee table. "Would you like tea, coffee, juice?"

She was pretending to ignore Arianne's worries. Arianne sighed. What was the worst that could happen if she went to Bible study? So Matthew might ignore her again, but what did it matter? She had Jeanette at gym, and she was sure Lucy would be friendly. Fine. She would go.

"A cup of tea would be lovely, Gran, but let me make it."

She watched both her grandparents open their mouths to object, and then close them again. Pa had brought a low table and set it up at the end of the kitchen counter, and they had put an extension power board so the kettle could be set up at a level where Arianne could make her own hot drinks.

"See, that isn't so hard, is it?" She smiled at them and wheeled over to the newly lowered countertop. Everything was in reach—the tea caddy, coffee, sugar, French press, mugs. "What are you having?" she called back to them.

"Tea. White with one." Arianne knew this information already about Pa's hot drink preference.

"Black tea for me." Gran sat down on the living room sofa, perched forward as if she needed to be ready to spring up to assist her.

"Relax, Gran. I'll manage."

Luckily the kettle was full, because she would have had to get help to fill it.

"We should put a spare bottle of water in the bottom of the fridge," she called.

"What for?" Gran asked.

"In case the kettle is empty. I can't reach the tap."

"Right." Pa stood up, went to the pantry, and retrieved an empty glass bottle. He filled it from the faucet and put it in the lower door shelf of the fridge. "Done."

"Thanks, Pa." Arianne stirred one sugar into his tea. "Since you're up, you may as well bring yours and Gran's tea over with you."

They didn't say anything, but it grated that she hadn't yet perfected the art of carrying hot drinks. They would need cups with sealed lids if she wanted to be safe and not get scalded by hot liquid. Or perhaps some kind of stable lap tray.

Something else to research. One step at a time.

———

"ARE you home for Bible study tonight?" Mom was sweeping the front hallway as Matthew hung up his jacket on the wall pegs.

"Not sure. Some of the guys are meeting at Jackson's place for Bible study as well."

"That's new, isn't it?" Mom asked.

"Yeah. I might go. Though I'm guessing the food will be better here."

Mom smacked his arm and laughed. "You're terrible."

"Why?" Matthew pretended a wounded expression.

"Always thinking of your stomach."

"No one cooks as well as you do." He kissed her on the cheek, aware that he was charming her.

"Given tonight's supper will be a result of everyone bringing a plate, you might not know what you'll get." Mom swept up the small pile of dirt into a dustpan.

"In which case, I might go to Jackson's place after all."

"Up to you. But we like having young people here as well."

Matthew went through to the kitchen and opened the fridge. Speaking of food, he was starving. This was the upside of still living at home. Other friends had moved away for college and set up on their own rather than returning to their parents. He'd decided remaining at home was cheaper. Besides, he enjoyed the closeness their family enjoyed. Though it was less now since Sasha married last year and Caleb had followed his girlfriend back to Australia. Mia came home from college in LA during term breaks, and Lucy studied in Walla Walla, so they were both often at home and he still enjoyed their company—mostly— unless Lucy was on a social reform crusade.

"How was your day?" Lucy followed him into the kitchen.

"Good. Yours?"

"This is my last semester of college, and I can't wait to be finished."

"You've enjoyed the courses though, haven't you?"

Lucy had a container of juice open and was guzzling straight from the carton. Classy.

"What?" She frowned at him.

Matthew raised his eyebrows and nodded toward the carton.

"You drink straight from the carton. I've seen you, so don't be so self-righteous."

"Speaking of self-righteous, I spoke to your disabled friend today."

Lucy frowned. "What do you mean, self-righteous?"

"After your tirade a couple of weeks ago nearly melted my face off."

"You're ridiculous. And could you please refer to Arianne by her name?"

"You only met her recently. Are you best buds already?"

"No. I haven't seen her since. Tell you the truth, I was so

embarrassed about the way we treated her, I'm not sure what I'll say when I meet her next time."

"You'll have your chance tonight," Mom said, as she breezed into the room. "And don't drink straight from the juice container."

Lucy replaced the carton in the door of the fridge without even a look of apology.

"What do you mean, we'll have a chance?" Lucy asked.

"Ruth Rayne rang to say her granddaughter is coming tonight."

Lucy smiled in his direction. Or was it a smirk? "What's that face for?" Matthew had some sandwich fixings on the counter and slathered some mayonnaise on a piece of bread.

"Round two."

"I will pretend I don't understand what you mean." He put the lid on his sandwich and picked it up for a bite, only just beating the rumbling in his stomach.

"That seems to be your style." His sister was relentless.

"What do you mean by that?"

"Pretending you don't understand, ignoring people who are right in front of you."

"For your information, I had a meaningful conversation with her today."

"Her?"

"Arianne Rayne."

Matthew had a moment of self-satisfaction as he saw surprise dawn on his sister's face.

"Just what do you mean by meaningful?"

Matthew took another bite of his sandwich. He hated being the focus of Lucy's interrogations.

"Just as I thought." She popped a small chocolate chip cookie in her mouth. "Pretending—"

"For your information, Miss Self-Righteous, Arianne

explained to me in clear terms how she felt about people who ignored and babied her."

Lucy's face broke into a grin and she finished swallowing her cookie. "Did she? Well done her. How did you feel about it?"

"Like a clown."

Lucy laughed. "I wish I'd been a fly on the wall."

"Just so you know, I'm trying to address my deficiencies."

"That's great news, bro. So you're going to stick around to meet her tonight?"

Was he? He still felt awkward. Worse—now he'd interacted with her—he was aware that he was a social klutz when it came to interacting with someone with a disability.

"Jackson is starting a new Bible study group for some of the guys, and I thought I might go there instead."

"That's an excellent excuse."

"Lucy!" Mom was still standing in the kitchen washing some vegetables in the sink. "I applaud your willingness to befriend someone new, but your superiority is a little overbearing. Can you let the rest of us learn as we go?"

A shade of red climbed Lucy's cheeks and her lips pinched.

Matthew felt a surge of shame. "For what it's worth, Luce, you were right. I did need a kick in the pants."

Lucy fisted her hips, triumphant. "Thank you."

"I will try to be more open to your sensitivity training in the future."

She tipped her head to one side and tilted an eyebrow and one side of her mouth up.

"What?" Had his comment been wise, or had he given her a license to lecture?

"If I were her, and knew you went out tonight, I'd interpret that as you taking the opportunity to avoid me. This will certainly reinforce her first impression of you."

Matthew took a deep breath. Lucy was probably right, but

he had genuinely talked about going to Jackson's place before he'd known Arianne was coming to his.

"Let's eat dinner and see how it goes."

"Dinner?" Mom was still observing the conversation. "What do you call that sandwich in your hand?"

Matthew smiled and kissed his mother's cheek. "I call it a snack."

She laughed, as he'd known she would.

CHAPTER SIX

W as this a good idea? Arianne felt nervous venturing out to a public gathering again.

"It will be fine," Pa said for the thirty-seventh time. "There are only a few families who come. No more than fifteen people."

Fifteen people including Matthew Kennedy. Why did the prospect of coming face-to-face with him have her stomach in a twist? Pa pulled his SUV up in the driveway of the Kennedys' house. It was too late to back out now.

"That was nice of them to keep it clear for us." Gran undid her seatbelt.

Not having to disembark fifty yards up the street was nice, but that didn't address the front porch steps—seven front porch steps, to be exact. It was something of a developing superpower for Arianne—being able to know how many steps and other obstacles stood in the way of easy access for someone in a wheelchair.

"Don't worry." Pa had read her mind. "I'll get you up without any trouble at all."

That was doubtful. The steps looked steep, and though Pa was strong for a sixty-seven-year-old, navigating steep wooden

66

steps was always difficult. She knew. She'd tried it a few times before.

"I hate to say it, Pa, but this will be easier if there are two people to lift."

"I can help." Gran stepped up, with her Tupperware cake container in hand.

"Knock on the door and see if James or Matt are there to help." Pa clearly wanted more muscle on the job. This was so embarrassing. Why couldn't her legs work? Why couldn't there be ramps and easy access wherever she went?

Gran mounted the steps and knocked on the door. She didn't appear to be offended that her strength had been called into question. They waited a few moments in the warm porch light shed from the carriage lantern style lamp mounted by the door. Arianne didn't know whether to be pleased or horrified when Matthew answered the door. He was a stupidly handsome man. But for the fact she was supposed to be getting over her relationship with Gavin, and she wasn't as free to jump into relationships as she'd once been, she would have been hopeful of attracting his attention. But this past week's encounters had taught her that all the attention she was likely to get from Matthew Kennedy was pity.

"Do you mind giving us a hand?" Gran waved in Arianne's direction.

Then he smiled. Matthew Kennedy actually smiled. At her. Arianne's stomach turned over. How ridiculous.

"Hi, Arianne. Nice to see you again." Matthew came down the steps and looked at her ... like looked at her as if she was a person. She couldn't help the smile that broke out on her face.

"Do you need a hand?"

"Can you grab the back of the chair? I'll grab the front." Pa spoke before Arianne had a chance to answer. The two men went about the task like she was nothing more than a problem to be solved, an object to be lugged up the stairs, and Arianne fought against shame. She wanted to yell. "I'm a person!" But nothing came from her mouth. What would be the use? How could they possibly understand? It was all she could do to prevent the stinging tears from making an appearance.

"Should I wheel you inside, or have you got it?" Matthew asked the question from behind, and Arianne felt a surge of gratitude. At least he'd asked.

"I wouldn't mind a lift over the threshold. I'll be okay from there." She hoped. There was no telling what sort of obstacles would be inside. Her chair tipped on its back wheels as Matthew pushed her over the wooden doorstep, and she was in the front entry hall.

"We're in the living room off to your left." He stepped away and threw her a smile as he led the way. Wow. He must have taken some of her talk to heart, though it was difficult to know. Still, she was here. If she could just get parked in a comfortable position, all she had to do was enjoy the fellowship and Bible study. It shouldn't be that hard.

"Arianne!" Lucy's exuberant welcome and hug felt good. "I'm so glad you could come. I was scared my brother had put you off us for good."

Arianne smiled. "We've had words in the last couple of days, and I think we might understand each other better." At least, she hoped so. Out of the corner of her eye, Matthew gave a small nod. She returned a smile. At least he wasn't ignoring her. Small steps.

Lucy helped Arianne into a position that was out of the way, so others could move about without obstruction. She brought her a cup of hot chocolate and a piece of cake. The cake—which she didn't need—was delicious. Still, she felt self-conscious. On one hand, she should be grateful that Gran and Pa were determined to lead life as usual—unlike the sheltered routine her parents arranged, which centered around her staying home. But with the normal routine came outside adventures and mixing with other people. Though she doubted they meant it, most people made her feel useless, an object to be got around. This was her new state of being, and she was going to have to get used to it.

"My mom is sharing the Bible study tonight." Lucy sat on the footstool next to Arianne's chair.

"I'm looking forward to it. I haven't been to Bible study since before the accident."

Lucy reached across and squeezed her hand. Arianne didn't know how to feel about it. Was that Lucy's expression of sympathy or was it empathy? Arianne didn't know Lucy well enough to tell the difference. But she did know she was tired of everyone feeling sorry for her. It was time to live and grow and engage with life—as far as her new circumstances would allow.

Arianne felt a sense of familiarity and peace when everyone was finally seated with hot drinks in their hand. Mrs. Kennedy welcomed the group, opened her notes, and began to read.

"Then Peter came to Jesus and asked, 'Lord, how many times shall I forgive my brother or sister who sins against me? Up to seven times?' Jesus answered, 'I tell you, not seven times, but seventy-seven times.'"

Arianne's heart nearly stopped. She should have thought this through. There were two things she wasn't ready to hear. One was healing—she'd avoided that conversation with Pa several times already—and the other was forgiveness. Gavin was in the front of her mind as Mrs. Kennedy read the Scripture, smirking at her. How could she forgive him for what he'd done? He was the one who'd driven recklessly. He was the one who'd walked away from the accident with nothing more than a couple of cuts and bruises. And he was the one who'd broken off their relationship the moment he learned she was unlikely to ever walk again. God had to understand. Gavin was a special case who most certainly did not deserve forgiveness.

"The thing about forgiveness is that it is usually applied to those who don't deserve it." Mrs. Kennedy's words cut into Arianne's thoughts. "None of us deserve forgiveness yet God, in His mercy, has made forgiveness available to all of us."

Arianne wanted to leave, to block out this subject. She'd heard it before—preached it before—but this was Gavin. He'd destroyed her life, physically and emotionally. This was too much. But she was going nowhere. Ensconced between Lucy on the footstool and Gran in one of the comfy lounge chairs, a coffee table in front of her, there was no making an exit from the excruciating sounds of truth.

"What do you think Jesus meant when He said Peter must forgive seventy times seven?" Mrs. Kennedy's voice continued, relentless in her oblivion to Arianne's emotional discomfort.

"I suppose 490 isn't the right answer?" Matthew asked. Arianne could tell he wasn't serious by the look of amusement on his face.

"I suppose it means to always forgive. That there's no reason not to forgive." This comment from someone Arianne hadn't yet met.

"Isn't there?" Arianne spoke under her breath. She had no intention of being heard.

"Sorry, Arianne. I didn't get what you said." Mrs. Kennedy smiled kindly in her direction.

Uh-oh.

"It doesn't matter." She ducked her head and focused her eyes on the Bible app on her phone.

"Please don't be afraid to share," Mrs. Kennedy said. "Sometimes it helps to chew things over as a group."

Arianne held her breath. Would the leader move on if she didn't respond? Now Arianne could feel the attention of all eyes in the room on her. Being here was such a mistake.

"It's just that the other lady said that there is no reason not to forgive." She nodded in the woman's direction. "That isn't my experience. I have a load of reasons not to forgive, and it's not quite so easy to just give them up."

Now she'd done it. An awkward silence descended. Arianne could feel Gran glaring at her.

"You're right, Arianne," Mrs. Kennedy said. "There are often loads of reasons not to forgive, and I guess that's the miraculous beauty of God-inspired forgiveness. Even to the worst of sinners, God pours out His healing power through forgiveness."

Oh no. Now she'd gone there as well. Healing comes after forgiveness. Just what she needed to hear. If only that were true.

"Sometimes it's easy for me to talk about forgiveness," Mrs. Kennedy continued "But I have to take into account that I haven't suffered at the hands of another in any significant way. My life and confidence haven't been seriously harmed by someone else's actions."

This was awful. It was as if Mrs. Kennedy was talking specifically about her. How did she know? Arianne cast a questioning look in Gran's direction. Had Gran and Pa blabbed about the accident and Gavin? Gran saw her and gave a small shrug, shaking her head. She hadn't said anything.

"I know the principle of how it works," Mrs. Kennedy went on. "It makes sense that forgiveness gives as much relief to the forgiver as it does the person being forgiven. But I can imagine how hard it must be for someone whose life has been destroyed. I guess I can imagine why they might not want to forgive."

Tell me about it. Actually, don't. Can we just wrap this up so I can leave and never come back again?

"I experienced one situation when I was angry at what a person had done. My life wasn't completely destroyed, but what had happened was wrong and there was a high level of disappointment and broken trust. I did not want to forgive this person. At all. But I knew Jesus's teaching. I needed to forgive, so my prayer became, 'Lord, help me to come to a place where I want to forgive.' I kept this prayer up for several months, still avoiding the person who had done wrong. Then one day, after a Christmas service, I saw the person, and realized my emotions had caught up with the truth. The anger was gone, and forgiveness had begun a healing in my spirit."

Mrs. Kennedy's story chipped away at the band of anger that held Arianne. She didn't want to forgive Gavin. She didn't want to see him, hear about him, have to acknowledge that he still existed in this world. But her love for Jesus Christ urged her to pray another prayer. *Lord, I'm so hurt and angry with Gavin on so many different levels, I could spit. I know that forgiveness is part of healing, and that you command it. On my own, I can't. Could you help me to come to a place where I would want to forgive.*

And just like that, a burden lifted. The burden of knowing that she was being disobedient to what she knew was right. It was as if the Holy Spirit had nodded her way and said, "I know you. I know your pain. Trust me. We will get to that place of freedom if you keep your trust in me."

Arianne became aware that the rest of the group had bowed their heads to pray. Someone had prayed, but she couldn't have repeated anything that had been said. Her own heart had been caught up in the warm hug of the Holy Spirit as she had yielded to Him.

I'm still not ready to forgive Gavin yet, but I can leave him with you?

Someone said, "amen" and the small gathering broke into chatter. Arianne took a deep breath, wiped a couple of tears that had begun to stream, and opened her eyes to those around.

"You okay?" Lucy leaned over and whispered.

"I'm fine." Arianne tried to sound blasé, but Lucy's eyebrows were still raised, as if she suspected more. There was more, but Arianne didn't know Lucy that well yet. "I'm fine," Arianne repeated. "God has it all sorted." That was a good Christian answer—an answer Arianne hoped was true.

———

PA AND GRAN didn't ask anything about how Arianne had felt about the Bible study. Arianne wasn't sure whether this was good or bad. On the one hand, the topic was swirling foremost in her mind. On the other, she wasn't sure whether a discussion about Gavin would end with her vomiting the negative feelings that had been with her since he broke off with her. They'd returned home, and nothing was said about the subject nor how anyone had responded to it.

Even when Pa drove her to the gym the next afternoon, he still hadn't said anything about it, yet Arianne hadn't been able to let the subject go. She hadn't realized how much Gavin's awful actions and the repercussions had been brewing below the surface. Last night's Bible study had punctured the seal she'd had over the memories and attached emotions.

"Good afternoon, Ari." Jeannette welcomed her with a smile, using her less formal name. It was nice to see that Jeannette felt comfortable enough to respond to the invitation to use her nickname.

"Do you mind if Matthew does your weights first, then I'll do some pool work after?"

Matthew wasn't in the foyer, so Arianne couldn't gauge how he might feel about the idea. But sure. Even in his clunky state, she'd be able to talk him through.

"Stow your gear, then head on over to the weights room. I'll let Matt know you're here."

This felt good. Jeannette was talking to her like she was anybody else, with no awkwardness or pity. Arianne put her backpack in the locker. She was already dressed for the work-out, so no need to change. When she arrived at the weights room, she found Matthew there with the glamour girl, Heidi. Arianne hadn't been much of a social media person before the accident, but with the reduction in her life since, she'd started the habit of scrolling. When she'd seen #MattK #TrinityLakes-CountryClub, she'd watched a few streams of Heidi's World. So not her jam. And if she had any ability to discern, it wasn't really Matthew's jam either.

But there Heidi was, her selfie-stick extended as she reached out with a tentacle-like grip to haul Matthew in. Arianne couldn't resist. She opened her app and clicked on the live stream.

"So, babes, tell Heidi's World how you think I'm progressing." Heidi pumped her other arm into a bicep pose, releasing Matthew for a short moment.

Matthew looked like he was squirming but forced a smile.

"As usual, a man of few words." Heidi kissed his cheek. "But he's a man of action, peeps. Let me tell you."

Ugh. Heidi was so slimy. She should leave the poor man alone and let him get on with his job.

"Uh. I have another client." Matthew pointed in Arianne's direction.

Heidi swung her cell phone around to bring Arianne into the shot but swung it quickly back. The look on her face told it all.

"I'll catch you in a few, peeps. I've got some killer hair products to share." She did her signature two fingers to lips sign-off kiss, and the stream finished.

Arianne rolled over toward Matthew and Heidi, then wished she hadn't.

"I told you to make sure she wasn't here when we do live streams." Heidi's tone was venomous and Arianne felt every barb as it sunk into her understanding.

"This isn't a television studio, Heidi, and frankly, your attitude stinks. Would you like me to tell that to your audience?"

Arianne froze in place. She was too close. She shouldn't be hearing this, but it was too late to back away.

"Don't get all self-righteous on me," Heidi said. "Just make sure my schedule and hers don't overlap. As it is, I'm going to have to go and edit her out of that clip. I hope there weren't too many people who saw her."

Matthew shook his head. Arianne felt an anger radiating from him that Heidi was oblivious to.

"I'll see you at church on Sunday." Heidi turned in a flounce and stilled when she saw how close Arianne was.

"Hi." Arianne put all her effort into a friendly smile, despite what she was feeling.

"Ugh. As if." Heidi stalked away towards the women's locker room.

Tears stung Arianne's eyes and she blinked them back. No. She should be thankful for this shift in focus. She hadn't thought of Gavin for a whole five minutes.

"I am so sorry, Arianne. That kind of behavior is unforgivable." Matthew wore a genuine look of concern.

"Unforgivable?" She forced a smile in his direction. "After your Mom's Bible study last night, I thought there was no one who was beyond forgiveness."

He studied her for a moment. Arianne sensed he was worried she would dissolve into a flood of tears. That might have been nice, but this was not the time or place.

"Let's get to work, Mr. Kennedy. I'm not paying good money to stand around moping." Arianne turned her chair towards the shoulder press machine, which was where she'd started last time. She pulled up at the forty-five-degree angle. "I can't wait until I've perfected the transfer enough to be able to do it without help." She smiled at Matthew as he arrived, determined to brush off the situation with Heidi. She'd done enough wallowing in the last year. No more wallowing. Time to live.

———

SHE'D JUST SAID, "stand around moping." She wasn't standing. Should he say something? No. Of course not.

He felt awkward about working with Arianne this afternoon. There were several things that had happened since last time, and he wanted to talk about them, but was unsure if he would be violating the Seven Pillars of Inclusion and would fall foul again.

Arianne detached the side piece from her chair and slid it under the bench. He followed the procedure they'd done last time, easily lifting her into place. That part of the process was easier now he knew what to expect. She lifted her legs into position with her hands and shuffled up against the backboard, ready to begin the press. She didn't say anything. Should he just set the weights and get her going?

He swung his leg over the long bench and sat facing her. On her level. She dropped her arms and he saw confusion all over her face.

"If this is insensitive, can you call me out?"

Arianne didn't say anything, but tears glistened in her eyes.

"Can we talk about the elephant in the room?" he asked.

"From where I'm sitting, there are a herd of elephants and I'm just doing my best to not get trampled."

"Am I one of the elephants?" Matthew found his heart in his throat as he waited for her to answer. He could see her swallowing, as if fighting down emotion. He'd wandered into a minefield, but it was too late to back out. "Will you forgive me for the way I treated you when I first met you at church, and after? I didn't realize how awful it must be …"

Arianne held up a hand. "Please, Matthew …"

"Call me Matt."

"Matt. I'm walking a fine line between my able self and my new status as a person with a disability. I never considered inclusive language or attitude or environment until I was the one sitting in the chair. I know people don't know how their behavior affects others who are different. I'm trying not to be thin-skinned, but ..." Her throat was working overtime, and a lone tear escaped down her cheek.

"I'm sorry. We don't have to talk about it."

"I ... appreciate ..." She waved her hand toward him, and the locker rooms where Heidi had retreated. "You know..."

Matthew felt his heart clench with sympathy. Should he show it? "I know. Seeing how Heidi behaves has educated me—that and Lucy's long-winded lectures. I'm learning, but it would be great if you could call me out if I'm over the line."

"Okay. Well, you're over the line. My personal trainer should not be sitting on the bench causing me to be emotional." She forced a watery smile.

Matthew smiled back and felt happy that the smile was easy and heart-felt. "Right then, Arianne ..."

"Call me Ari."

"Right then, Ari. No more playing soft. Let's get you doing some serious work."

CHAPTER SEVEN

The weights session went well. Arianne worked hard and was pleased that she could feel strength in her shoulders, arms, and even her abs. What she felt most happy about was that Matt was treating her like any other client, moving between her and others in the room. The only difference was that he assisted her transfers when necessary.

"How are you getting along with Matt?" Jeannette asked as she eased into the pool with Arianne.

"He's treating me like I'm normal."

"Great." Jeannette positioned herself to begin working Arianne's legs.

"I assume you had a word with him." Arianne moved her arms to get balance in the water.

"Words. That may be an understatement. His terrible start with you made me consider our whole business model, and how important it is to understand inclusion."

Arianne didn't say anything but allowed Jeannette to exercise her leg.

"I made Matt do an online course on inclusion in the workplace."

"Full marks to the course, because he's loads better."

"I've also decided I'm going to do an extra course on rehabilitation therapy. I'm really enjoying working with you, Ari, and I'm guessing there are more people who would come here if they thought it wasn't just a spa for the wealthy."

"It is in a country club."

"It throws off a prestigious vibe, and I'm sure that's what the owners want, but this community is small, and our current business plan isn't really inclusion friendly. I think it's time we reviewed that."

"I might be interested in doing the rehabilitation course myself," Arianne said. "I wonder if I'd be able to be a personal trainer."

"Why not?"

Arianne continued the exercises, enjoying the warmth and support of the water, and allowing her mind to consider possibilities for a future career in personal training.

After Jeannette helped Arianne from the water and into her chair, she handed her a towel. "After I help you get changed, will you be okay to sort yourself out? I'm leaving earlier to pick my kids up from school."

"Sure." It was awkward using one of the benches to get changed, and Jeannette had to help her still, but after that, she was fine to pack things up. Pa would help her into his vehicle as usual.

"See you next time?" Arianne nodded and waved as Jeannette left. She didn't wait once Arianne was changed and back in her chair. It felt good.

By the time she'd put her hair up in a ponytail and packed her wet things in her bag, she saw the time on her phone. It was near closing time. The gym sometimes stayed open late, but Jeannette said that was by appointment only. Country club members had a swipe card and could use the equipment at any time, but the personal training staff worked regular business hours. Matt had already turned the lights off in the weights room and was tidying things at the reception desk.

He looked up and smiled. "All good?"

"It's been a good afternoon." Arianne smiled back, genuinely happy.

"I'm locking up soon. Is your ride here?"

Arianne looked at her phone. There were two missed calls and a text message from Gran. Anxiety rose in her chest. Was something wrong? Two missed phone calls a minute apart was not a good sign. She pressed recall on Gran's number.

"Is everything okay?" Arianne felt breathless.

"Arianne. Thank goodness. Where are you?"

"I'm still at the gym. Where are you?"

"Pa and I went over to Walla Walla for an appointment this afternoon and intended to be back in time to pick you up."

"What's happened? Is everything all right?"

"We broke down about ten miles out of Walla Walla."

Arianne felt a surge of relief. At least they were all right. "Did you call roadside assist?"

"We did, but it's not good news."

"What?"

"We've blown the head gasket. We won't be driving the SUV anytime soon."

Arianne had a vague memory of a lecture about making sure that there was water in the radiator to prevent a blown gasket. Surely Pa would have taken care of such routine maintenance. But apparently not.

"How will you get back? How long will it take?"

"The tow truck will bring the car back to the auto mechanic in Trinity Lakes. I guess they'll give us a ride as well. Then we'll call someone to drop us out to the farm."

Arianne was glad they were all right and things were sorted on their end, but that left her sitting in the foyer of the gym with no way to get home. Did Trinity Lakes have taxis? In times gone by, she'd have used her app for a ride-share service, but even if there were any ride-share drivers in Trinity Lakes, they wouldn't have cars modified for wheelchair access. So were there taxicabs in Trinity Lakes?

"Do you think Jeannette would give you a lift home?" Gran asked. "She sounds as if she's a kind and helpful person."

"Don't worry about it, Gran. I'll figure something out."

Arianne closed her phone. She wanted independence. She wanted to be able to solve problems for herself. Here was the perfect opportunity.

"Everything all right?" Matt looked as if he was ready to leave and there were no other clients in the building.

"My grandparents' car has broken down and they're waiting for a tow truck."

"Can I help?"

"What is the taxi service in Trinity Lakes like?"

"Not great. We have one company that runs several cars, but I'm not sure if they have any specializing in ... you know."

"Wheelchair access?"

"Right."

"I can ride in an ordinary car. I just need some help in and out. What do you figure my chances are of finding someone who'd know how to help without panicking?"

"Good, I'd say."

"Really?" Arianne tried to hide the surprise in her voice.

"I'll give you a ride home. Given I've learned one kind of transfer, I'm sure you can teach me another, yeah?"

What was that jolt of warmth that exploded in her stomach? Inappropriate, that's what. But wow, had Matt learned a thing or two from his online course.

"Are you sure?"

"Of course. And think of the brownie points I'll earn with my sister and Jeannette."

"You've taken a beating from them, haven't you?"

"A well-deserved beating." He grinned. "No, Honestly, I'd be happy to run you home."

"All right then." Arianne wheeled over toward the elevators. "Are you ready to leave now, or should I wait?"

"I'll come up with you, if you give me thirty seconds to set the alarms and lock up."

Arianne hung back while Matt moved around and did the final checks, then crossed to the elevator and pressed the elevator up button.

They got to the parking lot, Matt clicked his key fob, and the lights of a gray truck responded. A smaller car would be easier for the transfer exercise, but this was better than no ride at all.

Arianne wheeled up to the passenger side and parked at the proper distance, set back from the front passenger door, facing forward.

"So how does it work?" Matt asked.

"Similar to the bench transfer." Arianne didn't detach the side of the chair this time. "First, put your arms beneath mine around my back and lift me upright."

"Probably should open the door first, hey?" Matt grinned, opened the front passenger door, and approached.

"Right, and I'll move the chair closer. And I should lock the brakes. Step by step instructions. We should make a video."

Arianne reached down and lifted each leg so she could fold the footrests up. Matt didn't try to intervene.

"What happens when you're upright?" he asked.

"Don't let go." This time she grinned at him. "Then help me turn so I can go backside first into the truck."

Matt lifted her upright as asked and held her. This was awkward. She'd thrown her arms around his neck, as was usual when doing this kind of transfer, and now she was in something that resembled a close embrace—and it felt good. Quick. Time to change positions.

"Usually the car is lower and you just gently guide me down."

"Yeah, my tires are a bit bigger than a car. I'm going to have to lift you."

Arianne began to think it through. This wasn't going to work from the current embrace position.

"Aahh ... whoops. I'm not sure this will work." Arianne felt blood rush to her cheeks. She wasn't in danger of falling, because Matt's arms were strong and secure, but it was still embarrassing.

"Do you have another plan?"

"I want to get to the point where I can use the slide board to hoist myself up, but I'm not there yet."

"In the meantime, I get to hold you close while we think of a solution, and while that's nice, and all ..."

"Could you just scoop me up and lift me?"

"What if I hurt you?"

"Doubtful at this stage, unless you throw me on the ground or something."

Arianne felt Matt change his hold to one arm around her back. In a smooth action, he scooped her legs up like a groom carrying his bride across the threshold. She hung on in a similar fashion. Their faces were in companionable closeness, and it would have been the most romantic thing ever if it wasn't so embarrassing. Poor Matthew. After all his bluster about not knowing how to deal with someone with a disability, suddenly she'd got him into this.

But despite all the earlier fuss, he managed the maneuver easily, even placed her facing forward, and made sure her feet were flat on the floor in the correct position.

"Well, that was tricky." Arianne pulled the seatbelt across and clicked it into place.

"How did I do?" Matt was still standing in the doorway and leaned slightly forward.

"You're a natural. No problems at all."

He grinned. "Wait 'til I tell Lucy. She'll have to come down from her high horse then."

"Don't persecute your sister. She's been so kind and thoughtful towards me."

"Now, what about these wheels? How do you fold them down?"

Arianne gave the instructions. Matthew stowed them in the back of his truck, then moved around to the driver's side, got in, and started the truck.

"I hope to get a car of my own eventually," Arianne said, once they started moving. "All I have to do is learn to transfer independently."

"Wow. I guess you won't buy a truck."

Arianne laughed. "A smaller car, lower to the ground will suit. I have to be able to fold the chair myself and stow it. There's a lot to it."

"So slide board transfer?"

"I've enrolled in a special course in Walla Walla soon to make sure I can practice the different independent transfers safely. In most cases, a person with an injury like mine would have learned the transfer before being released from hospital, but I had the complex shoulder injury."

"I'm learning so much, Arianne. I didn't have a clue about how it all worked."

Arianne shrugged. "That's normal. I'm just glad you've managed to see me as a person."

———

As a person? Was she kidding? He was beginning to see her as a woman. A very attractive woman. And now they had this whole close personal space thing going on, it was becoming harder to remain professional. Thank the Lord Jeannette had forced him to get over his discriminatory attitude and behavior. He still had loads to learn, but at least he and Arianne could now be friends.

They chatted about adapting cars for steering wheel control and other ideas that would increase Arianne's independence. The miles out to the farm passed quickly. Too quickly. Matthew was enjoying their time together.

"Sorry about our dogs," Arianne said, as they turned into the yard before the farmhouse. "They're slightly crazy, or needy, or something."

Two sheep dogs were straining at the end of their chains, barking furiously.

"This is a good deterrent for strangers." He stopped the truck and unclipped his seatbelt.

"And everyone else. They bark at all of us, even Gran and Pa."

"Maybe they are needy." Matthew got out of the driver's side and came around to help Arianne. By the time he arrived, she'd opened her door, turned out, and was lifting her legs to sit straight.

"Best set the chair up first. You'll have your hands full if you lift me first." Arianne smiled his way.

"Right." He retrieved the chair from the bed of the truck and unfolded it. She was so easy to get along with. Why had he been afraid to engage with her? He rolled the chair and positioned it in front of her, remembering to lock the brakes first. "All set?"

Arianne nodded and reached her arms out. He put his arms beneath hers and around behind her back and she flung her arms around his neck. It was an easy maneuver to turn her and ease her into the chair. Now what should he do? He could see a newly built ramp along the front porch. Was that all he was needed for? Should he go?

"Would you like to come in for a glass of iced tea?" Arianne finished placing her feet on the footrests.

Matthew looked at his watch. "Sure. Mum's expecting me for dinner, but she'll put my food aside."

"You call her Mum?"

"Right. That's the residual effect of having lived in Australia for five years while growing up. A few Aussie-isms slip in every now and then."

"It's cute." Arianne turned her chair toward the front garden gate.

Matthew wanted to race ahead and open it but didn't want to make her feel like he was smothering her independence.

"Ari?"

She paused and looked up at him.

"If you need me to help you do something, can you let me know? I don't want to leave you when you need help, but I don't want to stifle your independence. I'm probably saying this wrong."

She smiled, thank goodness. "Don't worry about it," she said. "Thank you for taking that into consideration. I'll ask for help if I need it, and I'll call you out if ..."

"If I step over the line."

"Right. And just for the record, I can open the gate myself, but it would be nice if you want to play gentleman and open it for me."

Matthew moved forward and unlatched the gate. "Just for your record, I've never been considered much of a gentleman—not from my sisters' point of view anyway."

Arianne moved through the gate, up the path to the ramp, and exercised some well-toned muscles turning her chair onto the ramp. Impressive. Should he follow her on the long route or take the steps?

"You can take the steps, Matt. I won't be offended." She'd read his mind.

He waited beside the front door while she wheeled up to open the door, but when she turned the handle, it was locked.

"Go figure," Arianne said. "I don't think I've ever been to this door when it's been locked."

"People do usually lock their doors when they are away from home."

"I guess they do. I've just never been here without Gran and Pa before. Hold on a minute." She took out her cell phone and placed a call. "Hey Gran ... Yes, I'm fine ... Yes, I got a ride home ... Matthew Kennedy ... Yes, Marianne's son ... Listen, Gran, do you have a spare front door key? ... Right ... No, don't worry, Matthew is still here. He'll get it for me ... Love you too."

"Where's the key?" Matthew asked.

Arianne pointed up to the eaves beneath the veranda. "Somewhere along the top of that beam. Now's your time to shine, Sunny Jim. I need your help."

Matthew laughed. Sunny Jim? Crazy girl.

Luckily, Matthew was tall enough to reach the beam under the porch overhang. He patted along the ledge until he felt a key, which he retrieved and handed to Arianne.

"Thanks, Matt. Let's see if I can actually open the door."

Matthew didn't say anything. He was interested to see how she managed and wasn't surprised when she easily unlocked and opened the door.

"Welcome to the Rayne residence" Arianne sat back and waved him inside first. It would probably have been easier if she'd gone in first, then he could have pulled the screen door shut as well as the wooden door. But ... this was her house.

"Ah, Matt? Would you mind shutting the screen door?" Arianne rolled inside and waved behind her. Matthew grinned. At least she wasn't afraid to ask.

"Do you want a hot or cold drink?" Arianne asked, as she opened the fridge and surveyed the contents.

"What's easiest for you?"

She turned and frowned in his direction.

"Right. I'll have a chicken and salad sandwich, and iced tea."

She frowned some more.

"Is that a 'no' to the sandwich?"

"Okay, wise guy. Let's make a sandwich, but you may have to help. I thought your mother was keeping dinner for you."

"She is. I was just kidding."

"Really?" She raised her eyebrows at him this time.

"Kidding about you making a sandwich. Not kidding about being hungry."

"Let's make a sandwich then. I'm hungry too, and who knows when Gran and Pa will get home."

Matthew followed Arianne's lead and her directions.

"Pull up a chair so we can work on the same level." Arianne pointed a butter knife toward the kitchen table.

This easy flow of working together was nice. Arianne was nice. The sandwich was nice.

"I appreciate you humoring me," Arianne said, before taking a large bite of her chicken salad sandwich.

This time Matthew frowned. "What do you mean, humoring?"

"Going above and beyond what's required for your job."

Matthew stopped chewing.

"What are you frowning at?" Arianne asked.

Matthew released a long breath. "I started badly. I really am sorry. Lucy was right from the beginning."

"You already apologized."

"Yes, but now I have to earn your trust."

"Trust?"

"That I'm really enjoying your company, not just trying to do the right thing to tick a box."

"Are you really?" Her eyes squinted as if she didn't quite believe him. Case in point.

"Sure. Besides, you make amazing sandwiches." He smiled. "I'm kidding again."

This time Arianne laughed. "I figured."

CHAPTER EIGHT

Matthew was glad it was Sunday. Jeannette opened the gym for clients who booked on a Sunday but allowed him the day off, given he was religious. He hadn't bothered to argue. He didn't feel religious—in terms of particular religious observances. His faith was real. He liked being able to attend morning service with his family and catch up with his friends afterward, but he liked to think his faith was part of who he was, at church, at work or at play. It had been a slap in the face to realize his faith had failed to influence his attitude with regards to Arianne and others who lived with disability. It provoked a deeper question: how many other minority groups had he ignored?

Too many deep introspections for the day. One crisis at a time, as his mother would say, and it seemed best he learned what he could in the current situation before searching deeper to find out where else he was deficient.

"There's a crowd of us going to the lake for a picnic after church," Lucy said as she climbed into Matthew's truck before service. "And I've asked Ari to come, so no going all funny about it."

"Give me a break, Luce. I've apologized."

"Well I'm glad, but let's see how you do when you have your friends around."

Matthew didn't reply. He hadn't put his new attitude to the test in front of his usual crowd, and hoped he wouldn't do something awful. Worse, he hoped his mates wouldn't be like he had been with Arianne.

There was an energetic atmosphere during the service, possibly something to do with the spring weather, and possibly a result of the sense of joy in the worship songs. Matthew was glad to see Arianne arrive with her grandparents. He'd considered asking to see if she'd like to sit with them, but they'd already settled in a place where there was space for her chair, and he didn't want to make a public fuss.

It wasn't until the service ended that Matthew noticed Heidi was sitting near the back of the church with a couple of other girls who, like her, stood out with their perfectly applied makeup and perfectly coordinated outfits.

"Who's that?" Lucy whispered, having followed his gaze.

"One of my clients from work. She's a social influencer." He should feel glad to see her in church, but he was more worried about what she might say to—or about—Arianne. Was he being too judgmental? Heidi wore an expression he'd seen before, and when she leaned over to whisper to one of her companions, a mocking smile on her face.

"She looks like she's in love with herself."

Matthew turned a frown on his sister.

"What?" Lucy shrugged. "She does."

"This from the person who has lectured me to a crisp for being prejudiced and unkind."

Lucy rolled her lips, and he could tell she felt his rebuke.

"Forget it, Luce. Have you made arrangements with Ari for after?"

"I sent her a text yesterday, but I'll go over and make sure we've got a solid plan."

"Great. I just want to catch up with Justin and Marcus, then I'll meet you after."

"Jasper and Logan and Tabby said they'd probably come, as well as Violet and a couple of her friends."

"Cool." Matthew moved out into the aisle.

"Is it okay if Ari comes with us in your truck?" Lucy slung her bag over her shoulder.

"Sure, if she feels comfortable."

Lucy moved away toward where the Raynes were gathering their things, ready to leave.

It had been a huge challenge, but Matthew felt a deep sense of satisfaction at having overcome his fear. He was looking forward to spending the afternoon with Ari, even knowing he had more to learn. Hopefully Ari would tell them how to make it work, because his imagination was struggling to figure out how Ari would manage at an outdoor picnic.

"Matthew." He looked up to see Heidi, batting her false eyelashes. He forced a smile.

"Hey. Nice to see you here."

"I've been before, you know," Heidi said.

He hadn't noticed her here before, but he wasn't going to argue. "No selfie stick today?"

"I didn't think it would be appropriate to bring Heidi's World into church."

"Right." Not appropriate. Not appropriate to let her followers know she had some sort of Christian leaning, or not appropriate to be causing a self-focused fuss in a place of worship? Either way, she was right to not make this about her. He waited a few moments for Heidi to introduce her friends, but she didn't.

"So, babes, we're headed down to the rowing club to do

some kayaking. We're going to grab some lunch from the Bell-bird Café. You can ask a friend if you want."

"I've already got plans after church," Matthew said.

"That's fine. You can cancel them. We need you."

"I'm sorry?" Matthew felt his hackles rise.

"Or ask your friends to come as well. The more the merrier."

"I think my friends are perfectly happy with the plans we've made."

"Yes, but I need you. My followers keep asking to see you somewhere outside the gym."

"Well, here we are, in church." Why did he suggest that? It wasn't appropriate.

"Don't be difficult, babes. Just ask your friends to come with us to the boat club."

"Fine. I'll ask." At that moment, Lucy and Arianne approached. Heidi had annoyed him, and he knew this was going to cause a clash, but he did it anyway. "Hey, Ari. Heidi wants us to go kayaking with her and her friends. Are you up for it?"

Suddenly the air froze with tension. Of course Ari wasn't going to be able to kayak. Lucy's look was thunder, and Arianne's face paled. Heidi frowned.

"She's not going to be able to come." Heidi didn't try to use a kind tone. "Your other friend can come though." She stuck out her hand. "Hi, I'm Heidi."

Lucy took the hand, but Matthew could tell she wasn't impressed.

"Sorry to disappoint," Lucy said, "but Ari and I have other plans. Matt can make up his own mind." Without waiting for a response, Lucy brushed past, pushing Arianne's wheelchair. Wow. This whole situation had gone from bad to worse. Arianne would hate being babied like that.

"Well, that's settled then." Heidi tucked her hand under

Matthew's arm. "Perhaps you could ask a couple of your male friends if they'd like to come."

Matthew untangled himself from Heidi's grip.

"Ah. No. Thanks anyway, Heidi, but I have made plans and intend to keep them. And just for the record, your treatment of my friend, Arianne, is ..." He paused. It was disgusting, but he wasn't sure he wanted to say that out loud in front of her other friends. "It's unkind. I'd prefer if you didn't drag me into your videos in the future."

He didn't wait for her response but charged out after Lucy and Arianne.

"Is everything all right?" Justin Perry, the youth pastor, stepped into Matthew's path. Great. He had apologies to make and there wasn't time to talk.

"Sorry, Justin. I need to deal with something. Can I catch you later?"

"Sure. Whatever, man. Your sister looked upset when she left a moment ago."

"Yeah. We're all a bit upset at the moment."

"I hope the Rayne's granddaughter isn't causing trouble."

Matthew stopped and glared at Justin. Did Justin just say that? He was a pastor. He should know better than to make judgements. "No, you can rest easy. Arianne Rayne is not causing trouble. I've gotta run. See you later."

———

"I'M SO SORRY."

Arianne could hear the sincerity in Lucy's tone, but it didn't make the situation any less awkward.

"Perhaps going out today might not be the best idea," Arianne said.

"Don't say that." Lucy pushed Arianne's chair up to

Matthew's truck. "I really want us to have a great time together. I can't believe Matt was so insensitive."

"Ah ... Lucy."

Lucy stopped pushing and came around the front to face Arianne. "Yes?"

"You pushed me."

Lucy's face dropped. "I'm sorry. I know I'm pushy, but I thought you'd like to hang out at the lake. Is it Matt?"

"No." Arianne took a deep breath. "You pushed me—pushed my chair."

"What?" Lucy's face was a picture of confusion.

"Like you took hold of the back of my chair and pushed me."

Color flooded into Lucy's face, and she clapped a hand over her mouth.

"Exactly." Arianne smiled at her. She didn't need to say anything else. Lucy knew. They'd discussed it before.

"You hate not having control."

"That doesn't sound great, does it?" Arianne said. "Let me say it this way. I'm trying to be independent, to have authority over my own decisions."

"I'm sorry. I didn't think. I was so upset."

"Yes, I got that. But can you imagine what it would be like if someone suddenly threw you into a wheelbarrow and wheeled you where they wanted without asking?"

Lucy covered her face with her hands. "I'm such a klutz."

Arianne moved her chair closer and put her hand on Lucy's arm. "We're all klutzy sometimes. Don't beat yourself up."

"Will you forgive me?"

"Of course." Arianne searched Lucy's face. "Of course, Lucy. Let's move on."

"So you'll still come out for lunch?" Lucy's face lit up with hope.

"I'm a bit upset with your brother, to be honest."

"I know, right?"

Just as she spoke, Matthew exited the church building. His look was dark, which matched her mood.

"Let me talk to him, Lucy." Arianne could see Lucy was winding up to give her brother a serve.

"Are you sure?"

Arianne frowned in a way she hoped communicated her feelings.

"Right. You're not a baby."

"Thank you."

"I'll go check on the others to figure out where we're going to meet. I'll be back soon."

Lucy passed Matthew as she returned inside. Neither acknowledged the other. Arianne took a deep breath. Why was life so complicated? Going out to lunch never used to be this hard.

Matthew came up and stood in front of her. Then he opened the truck door and sat on the foot board, putting himself more at her level. But he didn't speak.

Neither did she.

"So." He lifted his eyes to meet her gaze.

"So." She wasn't going to make this easy for him.

"That was stupid of me, wasn't it?"

"Pretty much."

"Do you think I'll ever learn?"

"There's always a chance, Matt. Especially if you can recognize your mistakes so quickly."

He gave a crooked half smile.

"Will you forgive me?"

"Yes, but I'd like to talk about the incident first. If that's okay with you."

He nodded.

"Do you understand what happened? Do you know why it was so upsetting?" Arianne leaned forward in her chair and rested her elbows on her knees.

Matthew nodded. "I think so ... actually, I know so. I knew it when I said it."

"Would you explain it to me?"

"Heidi was trying to finagle me into ditching our plans and going kayaking with her group. I knew what she was doing, and it annoyed me. When she told me to bring my friends, I just blurted it out."

"So you dragged me into it."

"I knew she'd be upset with the idea of including you. I figured it might get her off my back."

"Did you know how hurtful that was for me?"

Matthew rolled his lips together, inhaled deeply through his nose, and exhaled the same way. Then he nodded. "I knew, but I'd flipped."

"By flipped you mean ...?"

Matthew shrugged. "Said it without caring. And I hurt you. I'm sorry."

Arianne reached out her hand as an offering of peace. Matthew looked at it, suspended in the air, then met her eyes.

"Let's move on, shall we?" Arianne said.

He was slow to respond, but eventually took the hand she offered him. It wasn't a handshake, but more a clasp of friendship.

"Just so you know, I wouldn't mind going kayaking one day. Not sure if I can, but it might be fun trying."

Matthew lifted his gaze from their clasped hands to her face, sure the panic in his head must be reflected in his expression.

Arianne laughed. "Don't worry. We won't go today. But perhaps in the near future we could investigate how it might be done."

CHAPTER NINE

Matthew was on high alert the whole afternoon. A couple of other friends from church had agreed to meet at the lake for the picnic. Lucy hovered around Arianne like a mother hen, but Matthew sensed that Ari felt smothered.

"Want a milkshake?" Leah and Justin came up to where Arianne had been set on the grass while the others played volleyball.

"Sure."

"We're headed over to Becky's Coffee Cart. What flavor would you like?" Leah asked.

"Do you mind if I come for a walk with you?" Arianne used her arms to sit up straighter, as if she was about to stand up.

Worry jumped into Matthew's throat, and he moved over. Forget Lucy flapping around like a mother hen. He was just as bad, and he knew it. The look that washed over Leah's face was predictable. Arianne had asked to walk with them. Of course she meant go along with them, but it was another awkward moment.

"Ah ..." Leah looked around as if wanting someone to jump in and help her. "How do you get ... like ...?"

"How do I get into my wheelchair?" Arianne's voice showed she was teasing. "My personal trainer is well versed in how to transfer." She pointed to Matthew.

Well versed was an exaggeration, but he wasn't going to balk at the task at hand. He felt all eyes on him as he approached Arianne. "We haven't practiced this one. You'll need to give me instructions," he said.

In the end, he simply scooped her up from the grass and placed her in the chair. She picked her legs up and settled them on the footrests.

"Thanks, Matt." She beamed at him, and his stomach did a flip. "Want to walk along with us to Becky's?"

"Sure." He tried to pretend a casual response, and not like his heart was in his throat worrying. Worrying about how she would manage, worrying about how she would connect with Leah and Justin, worrying about how she would be able to order a milkshake. So much worry.

"Relax, soldier." Arianne spoke in a low tone. "I'm not going to fall to pieces." She turned her chair and rolled next to Leah and Justin as they waited by the pavement.

Matthew swallowed and forced himself to relax his bunched-up shoulders. He wanted to take the chair and push it, but knew she wouldn't want that, so he settled into walking beside her as they headed towards Becky's Coffee Cart.

"Thanks for asking me to come today," Arianne said without looking up. "It's been ages since I've been out just for fun."

"Tell me if it's inappropriate," Leah said, "but would it be okay to ask about your condition?"

Matthew's gut tensed again. That probably wasn't the right language.

"Relax, Matthew," Arianne said. "I'm fine to talk about it."

A quick glance showed Leah's relief.

"Thanks for asking," Arianne spoke to Leah. "One of the

reasons I've struggled to connect outside of home and family is because everyone is afraid they will offend me."

"It's scary. We obviously live a narrow life, as I don't know that I've had a friend with any kind of disability before."

"Friend? I like the sound of that." Arianne smiled. "However, it's likely you have a number of friends who live with some kind of disability, but perhaps not as obvious as the one I'm living with."

"What do you mean?" Matthew couldn't help asking.

"There are people living with learning disabilities, some with sight or hearing disabilities, others with mental health challenges or speech difficulties. I'm guessing you've had at least one other friend who lives with a disability."

"I guess you're right." Leah pointed towards the coffee cart. "Let me get the milkshakes. My treat."

Was that Leah's convenient way of avoiding a difficult conversation? He almost wished he'd thought of it. But Leah was an open and honest person. She would be genuine about trying to connect in an inclusive way. He'd best take a deep breath and lighten up.

———

IT HAD BEEN A LOVELY AFTERNOON, not just the weather, but having spent time with people her age. Arianne wanted to call them friends but was still cautious. Gavin wasn't the only person who had disappeared from her life after the accident. Other friends had withdrawn as well. Arianne understood—in a way. At the time she had been struggling with the worst news of her life, failing to understand she'd need to live her life without the mobility that had been hers all her youth and childhood. In hindsight, she knew she'd been emotionally up and down, and didn't blame her old friends for not knowing how to deal with her new reality.

She did still blame Gavin, however. He'd made all sorts of promises about their future together. Then, when he'd been the one to cause the accident through his reckless driving, he'd pulled back, then quit the relationship altogether.

Arianne shook her head. She didn't want to think about Gavin again. She wanted him forgiven and off her radar, not forever intruding on her thoughts and bringing up old pain. She sighed deeply. This forgiveness trip was hard work.

"You okay?" Lucy asked from the middle seat as they drove home.

"Yeah. Of course." Arianne forced a smile. She didn't want to put a damper on their afternoon.

"Thanks for coming with us," Lucy said. "I thought for a moment that we'd blown the opportunity."

"Me too." Matthew kept his hands on the wheel and his eyes forward.

"Listen, guys," Arianne tried to twist sideways so she could look at them. "We're all learning. If you can be open to discussing things, I will trust your heart that you don't intend to be offensive, and we should get along fine."

"Deal." Lucy grinned and held up her hand for a high five. Arianne responded with as much enthusiasm as her awkward angle allowed.

"You good with that, Matthew?" Arianne asked.

"Yup. I've come this far. No sense in backing out now."

"You'd better not." Lucy punched his arm.

Arianne's gut clenched. "Eyes on the road. Drive carefully." It just came out as a reflex. She didn't remember much about the accident, but she remembered the moments before, and Gavin had been casual and careless.

A stony silence fell in the truck cabin.

"Sorry, guys. These reactions just pop up every now and then." She hadn't intended to kill the mood.

"No, you're right. We need to drive carefully." Lucy placed her hand on Arianne's hand and gave a gentle squeeze.

"You guys are being awesome. Thank you." Arianne squeezed Lucy's hand back. "And speaking of awesome, I wonder if you'd do me a favor."

"What do you need?" Matthew asked.

"I need you both to come with me to a healing meeting."

The truck fell silent again, that awkward silence.

"I'm not actually sure I want to go, but Pa has been going on about it. I know he won't let up until I agree to go."

"How do you feel about it?" Matthew kept his eyes on the road, but Arianne could feel a genuine softness in his question.

"I don't know, to be honest."

"Do you believe in healing?" Lucy asked.

Arianne bit her lower lip. That was the six-million-dollar question.

"I mean, we hear it preached about at church often enough." Lucy sounded worried. "Of course, I think the love of Christ brings emotional healing as well as spiritual healing. And we see loads of examples of healing in relationships, and …"

"Take a breath, Luce." Matthew's tone was calm and confident. It was an odd change of roles. He'd been the one who was flighty and anxious when they'd first met.

Arianne took a deep breath. "In my mind, I believe in Jehovah Rapha, the Lord who heals. I know the theology, and I've seen examples—like you've said—of emotional and relationship healing. It's just …" She paused. Could she say it out loud? Matthew and Lucy were silent, waiting for her to relieve the tension.

"I begged God, like literally begged Him, to heal me when I first realized what had happened."

Lucy reached for her hand again and squeezed. Arianne could feel the sympathy flowing from her.

"Every morning, I'd wake up and ..." Arianne's throat swelled tight and her chin muscles turned to jelly. Tears pricked her eyes. It was such a painful memory, she couldn't speak. Every morning she'd tested her body, and nothing. Her legs simply would not respond. "He didn't hear me." A sob punctuated the statement. This was so embarrassing. If Matthew and Lucy were anything but true friends, this was going to be a disastrous finish to the day.

They had arrived at the farm, but Arianne wasn't ready to get out. She needed a moment.

"You don't have to go to the healing meeting, Ari, not if you don't want to." Matthew cut the engine and turned her way.

Arianne swallowed the lump in her throat and willed her face to stay positive, even forced a small smile. "I think I need to talk about it more."

"Do you want to go inside now, or shall we drive to the lookout over the lake?" Matthew's question was so thoughtful, Arianne was jolted from her own introspection. Who was this man?

"Up to you, Ari," Lucy said.

"I think I need to talk about it, but I'd better go inside before Gran and Pa explode with worry."

"Do you find your support team worrying too much?" Lucy asked, waving her hand towards her brother and herself.

"Yeah, but it's nice to know you care."

Lucy's smile was full of sympathy. It was okay. Arianne knew Lucy cared and wanted to be helpful and supportive.

"I'll take a rain check on that drive up to the lookout. And I'd appreciate it if you'd pray about my situation. I don't want to doubt God, but I'm not sure about putting myself in a public place where He can say 'no' in front of an audience."

Matthew undid his seatbelt and opened his door. "Are you sure God will say 'no'?"

Arianne wasn't sure of anything at this moment.

Lucy slid out of the truck after her brother while Arianne

opened the passenger door and used the hand grips to twist herself around. By the time Matthew arrived with the wheelchair, she was ready. There was no need to coach him now he'd figured out the routine. Without hesitation, he slipped his arms underneath hers and around behind her back. The lift and transfer was effectively done, except for the alarming reaction Arianne was having to Matthew's closeness. She enjoyed his physical presence way too much. It was highly unprofessional.

TRINITY LIFE CHURCH was hosting a week of services featuring a healing evangelist. Pa had pinned the advertising flyer to the fridge with a magnet. No matter what turmoil she was in, Arianne knew she would have to go. There were so many possibilities. Physical healing might be one of them. On the other hand ...

"The meetings will be from Monday to Thursday, just before Good Friday," Pa said. "Do you want to go early in the week or wait until Easter?"

It was no use telling him she'd prefer not to go at all. "Let's go on Thursday. Lucy and Matthew said they would come with me."

"I'm believing God for good things, Ari." Pa sat back in his easy chair and kicked the footrest out. His expression was satisfied and relaxed. Should she say something?

"Pa?"

"Yes, darlin'." He lifted his mug of hot coffee for another sip.

"What happens if I go and nothing changes?" Arianne watched his forehead crease.

"We've just got to believe, Ari. God knows our needs. He's powerful and mighty to heal."

Arianne didn't say anything. Those were words in a song she'd sung on many occasions. She believed it, didn't she? If she were honest, she knew doubt was nipping at the edges of her mind. She should shut those thoughts down and just trust God.

Easier said than done.

"Don't stress, darlin'." Pa seemed to read her inner thoughts. "Let's just go and see what happens. It's better to pray and believe and handle disappointment if it doesn't turn out the way we hope than not to pray."

That was a trite statement. It sounded good if she were talking about some other random person, but this was her who was hoping. The disappointment would be hers to handle when it happened.

Arianne excused herself and rolled into her bedroom on the ground floor. Without stopping to think about it, she pulled out her phone to call Lucy.

"Hi, Ari. What's up?" Matthew answered, sounding cheerful.

"Oh, hi. I thought I'd pressed Lucy's number."

"You did, but she's in the shower. She left her phone on the kitchen counter. When I saw it was you, I thought I'd answer. Is that okay?"

Was it okay? Did she want to talk to Matthew?

"If not, no worries. I can pass a message on to Lucy that you called."

"Have you got a few minutes to talk?" Arianne asked.

"Sure."

"Do you have the rest of the family around, or are you somewhere quiet?"

"I'm heading to the back porch as we speak. You sound worried."

"I am, a bit."

"What's worrying you?"

"I told Pa I'd go to the healing meeting on the Thursday before Easter."

"Oh, right. We're going to come with you, yeah?"

"What if nothing changes? What if God says no?"

Matthew went silent for a moment.

"I sometimes wonder if it would be better if I just accepted my condition and learned to live with it. This seems to be what all the naysayers refer to as false hope." Arianne felt as if she were holding her breath. Did she sound like a complete heathen?

"I'm not sure what to say, Ari." Matthew spoke slowly, as if he was measuring every word. "I've never been in your place."

"I feel like a failure as a Christian. I should have more faith."

Arianne waited. Perhaps Matthew wasn't the person to talk to about this.

"I've been reading some about healing and faith." Matthew spoke at last.

"And?"

"Some of it is cliché. It's all positive, and hoping in the Lord is always a good thing, but it seems like there are some people who want to push and judge. People who make cruel judgements about a person's faith if they're not healed. I'm not sure it's all good."

"I know. I've heard those sorts of statements, and that's why I feel like a failure."

"There was one preacher who said something sensible that might help." He paused. "Do you want to hear it?"

"I guess I may as well. This discussion isn't going to go away."

"He said, 'seek the healer, not the healing.'"

Arianne paused and tried to process the statement. She'd heard it before, and it could become cliche, but was there something in it?

"It's worth chewing on, I guess."

"I'm sorry, Ari. I wish I had the answer for you. This must be hard to process on your own."

"Which is why I was calling Lucy. I wanted someone to be a sounding board."

"I hope I haven't made it worse." Matthew's concern was evident in his tone.

"At this stage, it's all a whirlwind of questions, doubts, and worries. I don't think you could make it worse. I'm going to have to face it and face whatever God's answer is."

"You'll let us know if there's anything we can do to support you."

"Will you still be my friend if I don't ever walk again?"

"What? Of course! What a crazy question."

"A short while ago it wouldn't have been a crazy question."

"Let's not bring up my wicked past. Moving forward from here."

Arianne smiled. He couldn't see her, but it was funny hearing him talk about his wicked past.

"Anyway, Matt, thank you for listening. If I can count on you and Lucy for support on Thursday evening, that will be something, I guess."

"You can count on our support. We'll be there with you."

CHAPTER TEN

A rianne's heart was beating at a faster than normal rate. Her mouth was dry, no matter how many times she took a swallow from her water bottle. Everything inside was in fight or flight mode. Actually, only flight. She had no wish to fight.

"Are you ready, darlin'." Pa had his Sunday best on, his car keys in hand. Sunday best for a Thursday night?

"Gran's coming, isn't she?" Arianne kept watch on the stairs. If Gran didn't come, she would back out.

"Won't be a minute." Gran's voice floated down the stairs. "You two get in the car. I'll be there directly."

The opportunity to beg off drifted with Arianne's last excuse. Pa didn't seem to pick up on her anxiety. Either that, or he was so wrapped up in his faith and hope that he'd determined to press on regardless of any doubt or fear that might present itself. Should she make her doubt and fear clearer? Or should she just allow herself to be carried along by their expectations?

"Do you think I could try sitting in the back this time?" Arianne wheeled up and parked by the back passenger door.

"I guess we could give it a go if you feel confident." Pa

opened the door while Arianne lifted up her footrests. The back wheel arch cut the room down quite a bit, and the back door didn't open as wide as the front. Was it worth the extra hassle? The legroom wasn't as spacious as the front either.

"It's nice that your friends want to come along with you." Gran adjusted her seatbelt in the front.

Nice, and necessary. Arianne needed to have Lucy and Matt with her for confidence. Pa drove into town, took a couple of turns, and pulled up outside the Kennedy home. They could have gone in their own vehicle, but Arianne wanted them to arrive together.

"Hi." Matt opened the opposite side passenger door and hoisted himself in, sliding along to sit flush against her side. Lucy followed behind. Strange. Matt squirmed, trying to find the seatbelt latch tucked next to Arianne's leg.

A euphoric wave of something emotionally confusing captured Arianne's attention, and it took a few moments before she could gain enough perspective to respond to Lucy.

"How are you feeling, Ari?" Lucy spoke across her brother.

Honestly, she was feeling all in a dither having Matthew Kennedy sitting with his broad shoulders touching hers. It was so High School Musical, but that wasn't what Lucy was asking. A jolt, and she was back focused on their destination. Matt had taken her hand and given gentle encouraging pressure. She turned to look at him and their gazes held for a split second before he smiled.

Whoosh.

There she went—on a roller coaster of emotion that wasn't related to where they were going or what they were hoping for. She was behaving like a deer in the headlights, like a tractor beam was drawing her into Matthew's orbit. She was attracted to him. Like stupidly attracted to him. He was her personal trainer, and they were friends—now. He wasn't interested in her as ... as a woman. He couldn't be.

She was only a fraction of a whole person, and though he'd been working overtime to make her feel included, he wouldn't be able to cope with her whole self. Correction, the part-of-her-that-was-left self.

"We've been praying and fasting for tonight." Pa's words broke the spell. "I'm believing for good things."

Crash. The bottom fell out of her cloud, and Arianne hit reality with shattering clarity. The healing meeting. They were on their way to a healing meeting. Pa was expecting good things. Arianne was terrified that nothing would happen, and they would all come away disappointed. Especially her if she allowed herself to hope.

Hope.

She loved that word.

She hated that word.

Pa pulled up at the front of Trinity Life Church. Some of Gran and Pa's friends came to this church. It was a smaller, more traditional church than Trinity Lakes Community Church which Arianne had been attending the last month and a half. There was a white building with a stained-glass window at the front. And there were steps. Three steps. And no access ramp.

"Don't worry, Ari." Matt spoke in a low tone near her ear. "We'll get you inside without any trouble."

She didn't doubt it. Between them, Pa and Matt made sure she was able to access where she needed. It was still humbling.

Trinity Life Church didn't have a paved parking lot. There was some street parking, but the parking lot was muddy following a recent rain. There was no dedicated access space out the front, so Pa found a park at the back of the lot.

"We need to have a serious talk about accessibility," Lucy said in a firm tone as they all got out of the vehicle.

It didn't take long for her support team to get the chair out and ready. Arianne opened her door and turned herself outward ready for transfer. What was that disappointment when it was

Pa who reached inside to help her out and into the chair? Matt stood nearby and smiled at her when she chanced a glance in his direction.

"Are you good to go on your own steam?" Pa asked.

Arianne tried the wheels. The ground was nowhere near smooth.

"I could probably use a hand." She tried to inject cheerfulness in her tone, a front to hide her real feelings.

By the time they'd gone through the fuss of lifting her up the church steps and wheeling her inside, Arianne realized her attention had been diverted from her anxiety about the meeting to the embarrassment about the fuss her arrival caused.

"I'm so sorry." An usher with a name badge rushed up to Arianne as she took control of her chair. "We have an access ramp on the other side of the building. People in our congregation know this, but we should have thought to put a sign there for visitors."

Arianne silently repented of her earlier judgements.

"We've been raising funds for the parking lot as well," the usher continued. "We have plans for better disabled access. I'm really sorry."

Arianne smiled. It was good to know but hadn't saved her the drama on her first entrance this time.

"So good to see you here." An older lady came up to greet them. "My name's Olivia Darcy." She spoke to Arianne. "I'm a friend and neighbor of your grandparents."

"Nice to meet you."

"This is our last night, and it's been such a wonderful time of seeing God move in people's lives."

Arianne forced a closed-lipped smile. She knew what Pa hoped for. She knew what Gran hoped for. Now that everyone had seen her, she knew what everyone hoped for—that she would be healed. That she would walk again. She wanted to hope for that herself, but something held her back.

"Why don't we sit down the front?" Pa pushed Arianne in that direction.

Arianne grabbed her wheels. "Wait. No. Please, if you don't mind, I'd prefer not to be front and center." Pa stopped pushing, and Arianne took control of her chair.

"Over here." Matt found a space at the end of a pew near the back of the church. Arianne's heart was flooded with gratitude. Matthew seemed to be in tune with her tonight. And with that, the troop of butterflies took flight and tickled her inner being.

Stop this nonsense.

She was here to worship God and listen to a preacher who, by all accounts, had the God-given gift of healing. Arianne wheeled into the space and set her brakes as Matt sat on the end of the pew, right next to her. Lucy next to him. There wasn't any other room in their row, so Gran and Pa moved further forward and sat next to some friends. Was Pa upset or hurt by her resistance? Despite his enthusiasm, she wasn't ready to be pushed into a place where everyone was watching to see if God would heal her legs.

It wasn't long before the congregation had found their seats and settled. A small band with an acoustic guitarist, bass player, keyboard player, and a singer began encouraging the gathered congregation to join in proclaiming the goodness and faithfulness of God. The music was familiar. With the congregation in full voice, Arianne found herself drawn into opening her heart to God. Not so much to sing, but to close her eyes and allow her heart to begin to speak to Him.

God, I don't know why I'm here. I love you, but I'm scared being in a place where everyone is expecting a miracle. I want to ask, but what if it doesn't happen?

The music continued but changed to a Lauren Daigle song Arianne had heard many times before, "Trust in You." The singer didn't sound much like Lauren, but the spirit of the song reached out and wrapped around Arianne's heart.

Warm tears formed and ran down Arianne's cheek. Sometimes there were mountains that one could cry out for God to move, but even if he didn't, God's faithful and comforting hand was there. This was all she had. Trust in God. There was nowhere else to go.

God, help me to trust you.

Arianne sat embraced in the warmth of God's presence as the congregation around her stood and worshipped God. Finally, everyone sat down and were back at her level.

"You okay?" Matthew leaned over and whispered to her.

Arianne nodded. For the moment, she was okay.

———

THE VISITING preacher was full of passion and faith. If Arianne could just forget that everyone expected something from her, she could have listened to him all night. He spoke of faith in a loving God. He spoke of asking and believing. She'd done that, any number of times. But she wasn't going to go there right now.

"Sometimes faith is stirred by testimony. Let me introduce to you Chrys Webb." The preacher indicated a woman on the front row. "Chrys, will you come up here with me for a moment?"

A young woman who looked to be in her early thirties stepped up next to the preacher.

"Chrys, would you share your story of healing with the congregation?"

Chrys looked healthy and happy as she took the mic from the preacher.

"Thank you for the opportunity to share. I want to share this story of God's faithfulness of healing me from MS."

Arianne sat up a bit straighter. Multiple sclerosis. She'd met a few people living with MS. It was a debilitating disease.

"Symptoms began five months after I was married. I was twenty-one years old. They increased in severity, frequency, and duration until I was diagnosed two years later. We were told that if we wanted children, to have them quickly as I would be totally bedridden within ten years. It was suggested that we reserve a bed in a hospice."

Arianne's heart clenched. She knew what it was like to get such dreadful news.

"The next seven years consisted of long bouts of violent spasms and constant pain leading to paralysis, muscle weakness, extreme fatigue, blindness, depression, anger ... and three children.

Treatment was limited and I was placed on pethidine which did nothing for the symptoms ... but kept me quiet ... somewhat.

Though we were able to get a small disability allowance, we lost our new home to the bank. My husband was the only one with an income and rising interest rates made it impossible. We had to manage on our own, mostly. My husband worked two jobs and managed me and the kids."

Things had got tough for this woman. Arianne was thankful for God's provision in her situation.

"I was confined to a wheelchair, the three kids were at my mother's for the day, when there was a knock at the door. I eventually maneuvered through the cramped house to the front door, only to see two people walking away. Anger was my big issue at the time. It wasn't fair. I yelled and made a scene; they turned around and came back. It was two uniformed Salvation Army soldiers. They asked if there was anything that I needed help with, so in my anger, I told them.

They cleaned my house; did loads of washing that I couldn't reach from the wheelchair, but not once did they try to preach to me.

Salvationists came to my home three times a week after this, cleaning, bringing meals, watching the kids so I could rest. They organized for the two oldest kids to attend Salvation Army activities, even picked them up.

This began my journey to salvation and healing. Knowing God helped me deal with my anger and I coped better with my symptoms.

Though it took time, my husband eventually gave his heart to the Lord as well. Still struggling with mobility, I nevertheless joined the children's program at our church. I became so involved and enthusiastic about helping that despite pain and spasms, I pushed through, focused on helping kids who didn't have the means, to raise funds for a trip and camp. My parents were concerned I was pushing too hard and begged me to stop before I was completely debilitated. What I'd committed to seemed crazy and impossible, but I had a heart for the kids who were from welfare families and who had nothing.

Our last fund-raising event was a sponsored local creek clean-up. It was a hot day and I raced all day between clean up groups. My parents were at every road the creek crossed, yelling at me to stop before I ended up in hospital.

That night I realized that we had reached our fund-raising goal. I was so excited to testify the next morning in church, up early and ready to go when my parents knocked on the door. They could not believe that I was standing up.

That instant, I realized that God had healed me of MS. I had full sensation in both my legs; one of which had been shown to have 24% permanent nerve damage and the other 18%. I had no tingling, no pain, no blurred vision, full function... everywhere!"

Tears rolled down Arianne's face as Chrys finished her story. The young woman was beaming and praising God for his miraculous intervention.

"I have never had any symptoms of MS since that day. All my

nerve damage was restored, including the retinopathy in my eyes." Chrys beamed as the congregation clapped.

"Praise the Lord!"

"Amen"

Arianne couldn't help but add her own "Amen" to the chorus.

Let it be done, Lord.

"God works in people's lives whether they hear a famous preacher or not." The evangelist resumed his position front and center. "Through the work of his son, Jesus Christ, and the Holy Spirit, He desires to bring healing into people's lives, just like Chrys. What about you? Do you have a need? Do you need God's healing power in your life?"

There it was. The invitation to go forward for prayer. Arianne knew how it worked. She'd been to many meetings like this in the past. She could see Pa sitting ahead of her, knowing he was hoping she would respond. God wanted to bring healing. She should go. She should trust Him.

Arianne released the brakes on her chair and moved down the aisle. She wasn't the only one who responded. There were several people, everyone else walking on two good legs. But now her decision was made, Arianne was determined she would receive prayer from the preacher.

When she reached the line at the front, the preacher was already praying for people at the other side of the church. It didn't matter. Someone had set a playlist of music and a familiar song from Mercy Me played from the speakers, "The Hurt and the Healer." Arianne closed her eyes and breathed deeply. When the hurt and the healer collide.

Gavin. He'd literally destroyed her life. But had he? Completely? She had life, she had love, and she was sure she was on the way to finding purpose. Had he completely destroyed her?

God, Gavin hurt me bad. He should have been more careful. Why didn't he take responsibility? Why didn't he stay with me when I was so broken?

A well of emotional pain burst open and forced its way upward. She was human, and she was broken, but when the majesty of God's grace came in, when the power of Jesus's scars was understood, there was a collision. Her hurt and His healing collided in a miraculous explosion of light and warmth and power.

It's over now, Arianne.

She recognized God's voice.

It's over now. Let it go. Let him go. I am all you need.

An indescribable warmth encompassed Arianne from head to toe, and with it a welling up of compassion and love. Love for Gavin. Not romantic love. That was finished and gone. But a love that poured forgiveness into all her memories of him.

Praise God. Thank you, Lord.

The release from bitterness was like a heavy weight had lifted from her heart, from her whole being.

"Thank you, God." She tried her voice and found only a whisper available. "Thank you, God for your grace and mercy."

Suddenly, she became aware that the preacher had reached her and laid his hand upon her head. "God is already at work in you, isn't He?" Thankfully, he wasn't on the microphone and spoke only to her. She nodded. "Lord, finish your perfect work in my sister, by your Holy Spirit."

Arianne smiled. His work was done. Her heart was free. It was time to rejoice. And she did, lifting her hands in worship and singing along with the music.

CHAPTER ELEVEN

Matthew felt as if he couldn't breathe. Arianne had gone forward. She didn't look anxious. The opposite. She appeared to be fully immersed in her prayer, hands raised, face lifted toward heaven.

"Should we have gone with her to support her?" Lucy whispered to her brother.

"No. I think this is between her and God." He said it, but everything in him wanted to go and stand next to her, to protect her from disappointment. But this was God's territory. Arianne didn't need well-meaning friends getting in the way of her connection with the Holy Spirit.

The preacher finally reached Ari and laid his hand on her head. Matthew held his breath again. Lucy grabbed his arm and was watching intently. Would the preacher try to stand her up? Would she leap out of the chair and begin to shout praise? Lucy's fingernails dug in. She was as tense as he was.

Then the preacher simply moved on to the next person in the line. Something like a rock dropped in his heart. Nothing miraculous had happened. Ari was still sitting in the wheelchair, as she'd been when they'd arrived. Just as she'd feared. God had said "no."

"Is she all right?" Lucy whispered again.

Matthew didn't answer. He had no way of knowing. But she remained where she was, hands still raised and face still heaven-ward, even after the preacher moved on. Was she still hoping something would happen?

Maybe it would.

Eventually the church musicians returned to lead the congre-gation in a closing song, "Thank You for the Cross, Lord." Always appropriate, but Arianne was still at the front and nothing appeared to have happened. Matthew chafed with impatience.

The song finished and finally Arianne turned her chair. He wasn't sure but thought he could see tears. Any worry they were tears of disappointment was dispelled by the angelic smile on her face. The aisle became crowded as people moved to leave the meeting, and Arianne was blocked at the front. Why were people so inconsiderate?

"Come on." Matthew grabbed Lucy's arm and he excused and maneuvered their way forward.

"That was so good." Arianne spoke the moment they were close enough. "So, so good."

"How do you feel, darlin'?" Arianne's grandfather was ahead of them.

"I can't explain it, but God is so good. I didn't think I'd ever be free of it, but here I am. Light as a feather." Arianne's face practically shone.

"But is there any difference?" Mr. Rayne waved his hand in the direction of Arianne's legs.

"What?" Arianne looked at him, and her smile dimmed. "Oh. You mean ... the legs?"

Matthew watched, anxiety eating at his gut. A frown spoiled the radiant beaming of a short moment ago as Arianne appeared to inspect her legs. Tapping them, then wiping an imaginary bead of sweat from her brow.

"Sorry, guys. There's no change there." She cast a tired smile. "But, on the upside, I've just been healed of Gavin."

Gavin? What did that mean?

"Her ex-boyfriend," Lucy whispered in Matthew's ear. "The one who caused the accident."

Right. Matthew hadn't heard much of that story, only enough to know that Gavin would not be his favorite person if they should happen to meet.

By the time the Raynes had dropped them home, Matthew was still trying to figure out how he felt.

"You really care for Ari, don't you?" Lucy said, before they mounted the steps to go inside.

"Of course. Same as you."

"Are you sure it's the same as me?" Lucy raised her eyebrows with a knowing look.

"I don't know what you're getting at." He did, but now wasn't the time to open that particular subject.

"Matt. I love you, but you need to be careful."

"Careful about what? I've read the course literature. I've repented of being ignorant and stupid. Now what?"

"I think she's beginning to like you."

A punch landed in his gut. A hopeful punch. A "wake up and smell the coffee" punch.

"That's unlikely." Even as he said it, he doubted his own words. They might have started out rough, but their recent interactions had been smooth as silk.

"I think you'd better be careful, because if you don't have any intentions, she doesn't need another broken heart."

"Intentions?" Matthew could feel his stomach twisting.

"You know what I mean, Matt. Could you see yourself taking care of Ari for the rest of her life?"

Could he? Good gravy. Lucy sure knew how to drive a point home.

"Well, could you?" Lucy had him in a questioning glare that wouldn't allow him to move.

"I haven't really thought about it." That was honest. He hadn't thought about a long-term future with her. He didn't bother to clarify that he had thought about Ari—a lot. He had begun to enjoy her company, and he certainly didn't mind the stolen moments of physical closeness when he helped her transfer.

"For her sake, I think it would be wise if you did think about it. I don't want you to become another Gavin in her life."

Well, that was a slap in the face. Gavin. He wasn't anything like Gavin. Was he? Actually, he didn't know. He'd never met Gavin. All he knew about the man was that he drove recklessly, and he bailed when he realized Ari wasn't going to regain the use of her legs. Was he like Gavin? Had he subconsciously hoped that Ari would be healed before he admitted interest?

"Come on." Lucy led the way inside. "I didn't mean to upset you, bro. I just thought it might be wise to think it through.

"Yeah. You might be right." Might be? She was right. If he couldn't see Ari as a life-long partner, then he needed to pull back. It was time to do some soul searching.

———

IT WAS GOOD FRIDAY, and Arianne couldn't wait to go to church. Last night's encounter with the healing power of God had brought such a joy and peace she was ready to go and worship her Savior on a whole new level of gratitude.

Pa and Gran were quiet this morning.

"Tired from last night?" she asked as they set out for church.

"No. We're fine." Gran snapped the car visor up after checking her appearance in the small mirror.

They weren't fine. Arianne had a sixth sense about these things.

"It was a good meeting. Thanks for making me go, Pa."

Her grandfather made a monosyllabic sound and nodded.

"Are you sure you're all right?"

"We're fine, Arianne." Pa sounded tense.

There was something, and she worried it was about last night. About what everyone had hoped for—but hadn't happened as they'd expected.

Finally, they arrived. The Good Friday service always had a slightly somber tone, given its focus on the crucifixion, though Pastor Wilder was careful to iterate that the resurrection of Christ was a done deal. They didn't have to maintain the sadness waiting for Sunday. It was only a day of remembrance.

As the service finished, Arianne was ready to engage with her friends. Yes, friends. That was another thing that seemed to have clicked into place last night. Her fear of being rejected seemed to have been swallowed up in the confidence that the Lord had a purpose for her and she could trust him with how she felt. Evidence: the memory of Gavin no longer held any power over the way she felt.

"How are you, dear?" An older woman Arianne recognized from the Kennedys' Bible study approached her. "I'm Mrs. Wainscott. I met you at Bible study."

"Yes, hello. I remember seeing you there."

"How are you feeling after last night?"

"Good. Really good." Arianne cast a smile, though she saw the look of pity on the woman's face. She hated pity.

"Did you see any change in your condition?" Mrs. Wainscott pressed, oblivious to how Arianne's shoulders tensed and jaw tightened.

"If you mean physically, no, I didn't notice any change."

"I'm so sorry you didn't get your healing. Have you searched your heart? Perhaps there is unforgiveness blocking the power of God."

Arianne paused before speaking. There hadn't been any unforgiveness, perhaps for the first time in a long time, but anger stirred at this woman's words. Didn't she realize this was Arianne's own personal spiritual and emotional journey?

"Perhaps if you continue to seek God, healing will come later."

"Perhaps." Arianne didn't want to sound rude, but she wanted this conversation to end. "Nice to see you again, Mrs. Wainscott." She deftly wheeled her way past and headed towards her friends.

"Oh, Arianne. You must be devastated." Arianne was forced to stop as Kyla Ferguson stepped into her path. "Sometimes you just need to have more faith."

"Thank you, Kyla, for your encouragement. Actually, I had an amazing encounter with God. Oh, look, Lucy's calling me. I'll catch you later."

She wheeled away, but her heart of thankfulness and praise had been seriously undermined.

Arianne moved directly towards where Lucy was talking to Elissa Bennet.

"Hi." Lucy smiled and stood back to include Arianne in the circle.

"How are you?" Elissa had an Australian accent. Arianne hadn't spoken to her before, even though she knew who she was.

"That service was so moving," Arianne said. "I don't know if it's just me, but I can't help but be grateful for the grace of God."

"It was a good service," Elissa agreed. "This is my first Easter at Trinity Lakes."

"But not your last." Lucy waggled her eyebrows.

"Liam and I will be getting married later this year." Elissa turned to Arianne. "Then I will be an official resident of Trinity Lakes."

"Part-time resident," Lucy said. "I'm not sure if you've met Liam, but he's an entrepreneur and splits his time between here and Seattle."

"And other places in the world," Elissa added.

"You're from Australia?" Arianne asked.

Elissa nodded. "I've been here in the US just over a year. Started studying as a post-grad student at Seattle University, met Liam, won a scholarship, and will be finishing up a research project just before we get married."

"I'd love to go to Australia one day."

"You should go." Elissa's face was animated.

"We'll be going sometime soon," Lucy said. "Caleb and Alanah will be getting married eventually, and we'll be invited to their wedding Down Under."

"I'd heard they were finally engaged. About time." Elissa turned and welcomed a tall handsome man. By the way they connected in a side embrace, Arianne guessed this was Liam.

"Are you ready to go?" Liam directed the question to Elissa.

"Did you meet Arianne?" Elissa asked. "This is my fiancé, Liam."

"Nice to meet you." Liam reached out his hand and Arianne took it. "Sorry to split up your conversation, but Gran is expecting us for lunch."

"See you Sunday." Elissa gave a small wave to both of them, and they moved off.

"You didn't answer Elissa's question." Lucy turned to full face Arianne.

"What question?"

"How are you?"

"I'm good." Arianne frowned. "I just told you I really enjoyed the service."

"Yes, but after last night?"

Arianne took a deep breath. This was why everyone was acting strangely. They were worried about her disappointment.

"Are you free for lunch?" Arianne asked.

"Of course."

"Matt?"

"Not sure about him. He said something about going out with some mates."

"Oh." There was a sinking feeling.

"But we can go out to the Bellbird or something."

"Sure. That will be great. Should I have Pa drop me off there? Do you want to ride with us?"

Lucy smiled. "Believe it or not, I do have a license."

"But do you have a car?"

"Well, not actually. Not while I'm still studying. But I'm sure Dad will lend me his car, if we drop them home first."

It took a bit of arranging, but eventually, Lucy was able to help Arianne transfer, and finally get seated at a café table.

"Everyone is acting strange today." Arianne moved her drinking glass around in a small circle. Lucy didn't reply. "It's because I went forward for prayer and there hasn't been any physical change."

"We're worried about it."

"We?"

"I guess everyone, but I'm worried about it. Aren't you disappointed?"

Arianne fiddled with the table fork. Was she disappointed? She had blocked the idea from her mind, and that hadn't been hard given the warmth of the miracle that *had* occurred. But when everything settled down, and Arianne came face to face with the question, she had to admit that it was an ongoing struggle to accept the situation for what it was. God had healed her heart. If He wanted to heal her body as well, then she would be ready for it. But she was going to do as Matt had reminded her, to seek the healer more than the healing.

"Ari?" Lucy spoke softly.

"It's just how it is. I have to accept it."

"Some people think ..."

"I don't really want to know what people think, if I'm honest. I've already heard from several this morning who were giving me advice on how I should pray harder or believe harder or forgive more. It's not their business how I connect with God, Lucy."

Lucy fell silent. Had that been harsh? "Listen, I'm sorry. I'm open if God has full healing in His plan, but in the meantime, I can't manipulate healing into being. I have to get on with the life I have."

"You're right. I'm sorry." Lucy picked up the menu.

"What do you want to eat?" Arianne asked.

"Hot cross buns."

Arianne looked at the words on her menu. "What are hot cross buns?"

Lucy put the menu down and looked up. "Seriously? It's Good Friday, and the tradition is to eat hot cross buns."

"Can't say that I've ever heard of them." Arianne said.

"You can't eat anything else in Australia at Easter time. The warm, fruity, cinnamon yeast buns with a piped cross on top. Hot cross buns bring back such great memories of when I lived there as a kid."

"And this café is Australian themed, yeah?" It was hard to miss with the map of Australia and the Australian flag on the corners of the menu.

"Hence why I love coming here. So are you up for an Aussie Easter tradition?"

"Fine. Let's eat hot cross buns." Arianne smiled as Lucy went to order at the counter.

CHAPTER TWELVE

Matthew hadn't connected with Arianne in several days. She'd been at the Easter services and he'd seen her across the sanctuary, but hadn't actively sought her out. Lucy's words had bothered him. What were his intentions?

It was too soon for that question. He was still in the attraction zone. Now that he was called to think about it, his thoughts were more a question. How did he feel about her? Well, that wasn't hard. He liked her. Once he'd got past the awkwardness, he'd found her fascinating. But fascination wasn't a good basis for a relationship. Yes, she was an attractive woman. No doubt about that.

But she was living with disability, and no matter how ableist it might be, what did that mean in terms of a serious relationship? Well, he *was* serious already, but was he *that* serious? For better, for worse, in sickness and in health? He'd mastered the car transfer and other simple transfers. She had aspirations of being independent enough to do transfers herself, and he didn't doubt that she would achieve it. What else was there to know? Because Lucy was right. If he excited interest in her and she began to get attached, then he came to a place where he felt it was all too hard, it would be worse than what Gavin had done.

Was his hesitation because he'd hoped for full physical healing? A moment of honesty annoyed him from behind. He had hoped, and he'd felt disappointed on her behalf. But if he was honest, he knew he'd been disappointed on his own behalf as well. That was terrible. Horrible. He was a horrible person. A horrible, shallow, ableist person.

God, help me. I need to sort my heart out. This was so wrong.

"Are you working with Ari today?" Jeanette looked down the list of booked clients.

"Ah. Could you work with her today?"

"Why?" Jeanette pinned him with a glare.

"I … it's just that …"

"Matthew Kennedy, what have you done?"

"What makes you think I've done anything?"

"Because you're hedging again. What's the problem now?"

"There isn't a problem. I've been hanging out with her for several weeks."

Jeanette held his gaze, her eyes sparking and her jaw tense.

"I just think it would be best if there was some distance." Matthew didn't want to admit to the thoughts that had been troubling him.

Jeanette pressed her lips together and took a deep breath. "This had better not be something to do with that social influencer woman."

"Heidi? No. She's got nothing to do with it."

"She'd better not." Jeanette moved around and picked up the tablet, opening the screen and reviewing. After scrolling for a moment, she turned her attention back to him. "I can do the pool work, but you'll have to do the weights as usual. I've got another pool client straight after."

Matthew nodded. He'd done his best without confessing the

depth of his worry. What he needed to do was pray for wisdom. He did not want to hurt Arianne.

———

ARIANNE COULDN'T WAIT to see Matt again. She was full of enthusiasm given the news she'd received.

"Hey, stranger." She rolled into the weights room and set herself at the first station ready for transfer. "Missed catching up over Easter. Did you have a good one?"

Matt nodded. "It was quiet, but good. What about you?"

"After Thursday night, I was so excited, given the healing I received."

"Healing?" He looked up, definite surprise evident.

She disconnected the side piece of her chair and handed it to him. "The weight I've been carrying around since Gavin left was wearing me down. Remember? It feels so good to be free."

Matt didn't respond. Odd.

"You okay?" She asked as he pulled her forward and put his arms around her back.

"Sure." This was unusual. What was bothering him?

Once she was set on her first machine, he stood back. "I'll let you follow the routine and get back to you shortly."

Arianne took hold of the shoulder presses and watched him walk over to another client. Why did she feel as if he was shutting her out? Because he was shutting her out—which he hadn't done since he'd done that online course. What was the matter? She applied herself to the reps, and then waited for him to circulate around to help her shift to the next machine.

"I've had some good news." Despite feeling this distance, Arianne was determined to break the wall that had come between them.

"That's good." He helped her transfer and move to the bench press.

"Are you interested in knowing what the news is?" His apparent indifference was making her anxious. Surely he wouldn't revert to the way he'd been when they'd first met.

"Sure." There was no conviction in his tone, and Arianne's heart sank.

"That's okay. I can see you're distracted. We can talk another time."

Matt gave an unconvincing smile, then turned and left.

There was something wrong. That wasn't hard to see, and it wasn't hard to conclude that he had a problem with her. Was it because of Thursday night? Was he like everyone else, disappointed because she hadn't been healed? He'd been so understanding and supportive before the meeting. This was so hard to figure out. She might have been dealing with the outcome of Thursday night well, but Matt's attitude was a whole lot harder. She'd begun to consider him as one of her friends, a title she'd held back from giving people because of what had happened after the accident.

Arianne took the small barbells and worked with them according to the usual program, but she wouldn't be able to do the bench press until Matt returned to spot for her.

"Could you please tell me what's going on?" Arianne asked when he returned to her.

He didn't try to deny it—to his credit—but he didn't explain himself either, breathing out through his nose.

Arianne wasn't going to drag this out of him but kept her focus on him until he finally acknowledged her.

"Could we talk after work?" Matt asked. The look on his face showed he was worried.

"I'll get Pa to drop me at the Bellbird Café after and wait around, if that's okay?"

Matt nodded, then stood behind the bench, adjusting the weights. Fine. She would do her program, call Pa, and ask if it was okay for him to drop her into Main Street for a bit. She would wait for her "friend" to explain what was going on.

———

JEANETTE WAS STAYING LATER this afternoon, so Matthew checked he'd finished all his paperwork, gathered his bag, and headed to the elevator.

"I'll see you tomorrow." Jeanette called as he went by. "Hopefully you will have figured out what's eating you by that time."

Matthew gave a weak smile, waved, and entered the elevator. He knew exactly what was eating him. Was he ready for a committed relationship? A life-long relationship? This wasn't some light dating situation where they could have some laughs for a few months, then decide to move on to someone else. Arianne's story of rejection made the question even more important. If he was certain of one thing, it was that he cared enough for her not to thoughtlessly hurt her.

Matthew parked his truck two blocks away and decided to walk to the Bellbird. He needed the exercise, fresh air, and time to pray. *God, help me find the right thing to say.*

As he was walking past Cohen's hardware store, Jasper was loading building supplies into the back of his truck.

"Hey." He waved a greeting to his mate from school. "Looks like a serious project."

Jasper returned a half-hearted smile. "I'm keeping busy."

"How's Ellie?" Ellie Reilly was one of Jasper's best friends who'd been in Europe since New Years Eve.

"Yeah, she arrived back home last week, just before Easter."

Matthew could sense a sadness in Jasper's tone. "I thought you and she might have ..." Matthew shrugged his shoulders ... "You know. I thought you really liked her, and now that she's back from her trip ..." He shrugged again.

"Yeah. I like her, and she likes me. We're in a lovely friend-zone situation."

"Right." Matthew could relate to Jasper's problem. "I'm sensing you'd like more but perhaps she's not as keen?"

"I hate the friend zone. I'm in a complete knot. I want to tell her straight out, but all she can talk about is how great it was in France, and Ellie ... Well, you don't need to know all my relationship drama."

In fact, it was great hearing Jasper's relationship drama. It diverted his thoughts from his own for a few moments.

"I guess I'll catch up with you at football training later this week," Matthew said.

"Right." Jasper smiled. "I've been recruited for Team USA. I assume you'll still be playing for the Aussie team."

"Five years of school in Australia is hard to get out of the system."

"That's an advantage, five years of playing AFL before. I'm still struggling to figure the game out." Jasper shut the tailgate of his truck.

"It's one of the best sports on the planet," Matthew said. "I wish it was played professionally here in the States."

"Whatever. If I run around and get tackled a few times, it might keep my mind off Ellie for five minutes."

"Sorry, mate. I sympathize."

"You got women troubles as well?"

"I'm not sure. Maybe. I'm on my way for a coffee date as we speak."

"Good luck."

"You too."

Matthew waved to Jasper and continued, crossing the road to the Bellbird Café. The Aussie-themed café was often frequented by Aussie expats. He was American born, but he'd spent enough of his childhood in Australia and New Zealand to love the vibe.

It wasn't hard to spot Arianne. She'd found a spot by the front window. He flicked a look at his watch. It was getting on toward dinnertime. He should have thought about that. But he wanted to explain. He wasn't sure how, but his coldness was unkind. He knew that.

"Hey, Ari."

She looked up from the book she was reading as he approached and offered him a smile. It wasn't as brilliant as the other night—a solid fifty percent less dynamic. That was his fault. He pulled out a chair and sat down adjacent to her, also having a view of the street. The afternoon light was fading fast.

"I'm sorry it's so late. I didn't think about that."

"Don't worry about it." Arianne's face was a question. She wanted answers.

"Are you sure you don't need to get home for dinner?"

"I think I'd prefer to have this talk, if that's okay with you."

Matthew straightened in his chair and took a deep breath.

"What's wrong, Matt?" Arianne's tone was gentle.

"I don't quite know how to explain it."

"Is this about me and the healing meeting?"

Matthew's head shot up. "Partly."

Arianne's lips disappeared and he could see she also was struggling with something.

"I don't want to hurt you, Arianne. I'm scared I'm going to hurt you worse than what Gavin did."

"Why would you think that?" Her brow furrowed.

Matthew took another deep breath. It didn't matter which way he framed it, it sounded bad.

"Matthew?" She leaned closer, her gaze searching his.

"I care about you, I really do. As a friend."

She drew back slightly and gave a small nod. "I know." She took a deep breath.

"It's just that Lucy said … I mean … she thought you might want more than friendship."

"I've never said a word about you to her." Now Arianne sounded defensive.

"I don't want to be egotistical. I was just going by what Lucy said."

"That's fine, Matt. I understand. We are friends. Nothing more."

Matthew held eye contact for a bit longer. Her eyes were shining with tears. She said she understood, but did she? He wasn't sure he understood.

"I'll call Pa and have him pick me up."

"No, that's fine. I'll drop you home." Matthew didn't feel as if he'd clarified things at all. There was so much still left that hadn't been discussed. They were friends at the moment, but he needed to consider if their relationship was going to become more.

Ari packed her book in her backpack, finished the dregs of the coffee sitting in front of her, and pushed back from the table. Matthew hadn't had time to order anything, but his emotional quandary had stolen his appetite in any case.

As they wheeled into the street, Arianne turned to look at him. "Where's your truck?"

"I parked a couple of blocks away. Sorry. Do you mind wheeling that far? Or you could wait while I run and get it."

"It's a nice evening for a short stroll. I'll roll along with you."

Matthew wasn't sure whether to be relieved or worried. Relieved that she was happy to spend more time in his company, worried about all the other things still brewing beneath the surface.

"You said you had some good news earlier? Want to share?" Matthew was glad he remembered.

"Yeah. I was quite excited about it. Adam Lancaster, you know him right?"

"Your PT. Yeah. Of course."

"He's really positive about how the exercises we've been

doing are beginning to show new neural pathways are developing."

"What does that mean?"

"I may be able to learn to stand up and move with walking aids, in time."

"Wow. Really?"

"Well, I don't know if it will work, but I have been able to move a couple of toes every now and then. That's a good sign."

"That's fantastic, Arianne."

"The only thing is, before I go to one of the rehabilitation hospitals to see if we can get something like this going, I need to make sure my shoulder has healed enough to support me standing with a mobility device. I don't want my arm to give out and fall. I'm hoping it's all good and there won't be any need for further surgery."

Matthew's chest constricted. He didn't want Arianne to suffer more. He wanted her to be well. At least, as well as she could be.

"What will you do if they want to do more surgery?"

"Pray about it, I guess."

That was a brave statement, considering what hadn't happened on Thursday night.

"How did you feel about the healing meeting?"

"I'm not going to pretend I don't know what you're asking. Nobody has hidden their disappointment that I didn't get out of my chair and start jumping about."

"I saw how much you were affected by God's healing, Arianne. I know you were released from something. You were beaming."

"But I wasn't walking."

"No."

"Are you asking how I feel about that?"

Matthew could only see Arianne in his peripheral vision as

they moved along side by side. But he saw the emotion on her face.

"I wanted to walk, Matthew. Of course I wanted to walk, and run, and play sports again. It's who I was before the accident."

"I'm sorry."

She let out a heavy sigh. "So am I. But I asked. God has said 'no.'"

"How do you feel about God?"

"I need Him too much. What He's done in my heart is too great for me to cut Him off because He hasn't answered my prayer the way I wanted Him to."

"You're very brave."

"Not as brave as you think. I lie awake crying at night." They had reached his truck and he turned to look at her.

"Do you?"

"In the first few months, that was most of my life—crying out 'why me?' Now, it happens every now and then."

"Like the other night?"

"I was on too much of a high after the meeting to realize what hadn't happened, only what had. It hit me more after the Good Friday service when half the congregation decided to remind me that God had denied my request for healing and gave me all kinds of unsolicited advice on how I should be more spiritual."

"I'm sorry, Ari."

"And you decided to go AWOL."

Matthew felt a punch in his gut.

"Even Pa couldn't hide his disappointment. That I'd experienced God's emotional healing was wonderful, but the realities of life and expectations soon came to dump on me. I've done plenty of crying."

An overwhelming desire to pick her up and hold her in his arms flooded his heart. They were at the truck. He would pick her up, he would hold her, if only for a moment. With the door open and her ready, he lifted her upright, her arms flung around his neck, as usual, but before scooping her up, he stopped and looked into her eyes. "I'm really sorry, Arianne. Truly, I am."

"I know." Her eyes held his. For a suspended second his whole being urged him to kiss her, but Lucy's words held him back. He'd said friends. Friends didn't go about kissing each other. If he crossed that line, he knew that it was either commit to her for the rest of his life, or break her in a way that made Gavin seem like an angel.

He scooped her up and deposited her safely in the passenger side of his truck. They were friends. For the moment, that was going to have to suffice.

CHAPTER THIRTEEN

Just friends. What a horrible, soul-destroying mantra to have to repeat over and over, day in, day out. Just friends. Arianne could see Matt cared about her, but he wasn't professing undying love. He cared about her as a friend. Although, if she was any judge of body language, she could have sworn his hold on her the other night was radiating emotional energy, and that the urge to kiss wasn't only on her side. But he hadn't kissed her. He'd deposited her into his truck in a careful and friendly manner.

Just friends.

Arianne determined to put it from her mind. He was right, of course. He had the potential to hurt her in a way that was far more devastating than how Gavin had hurt her. Lucy was astute. She had called it. She had warned him. He was being careful.

Just friends.

"I think I'm ready for the next step in rehabilitation," Arianne announced as she wheeled up to the breakfast table.

"What's the next step, darlin'?" Pa took a swig of coffee.

"I'm going to consult a specialist in Spokane to ask if he

thinks my shoulder might be ready to bear the weight of me relearning to walk."

"Will you do that when you do those workshops on slide board transfers?" Gran placed a plate of toast on the table in front of Arianne, then sat down beside her.

"Yes. I was going to do the slide board sessions in Walla Walla, but since I need to go to Spokane to see the specialist, I'm going to do it all at once. My PT believes I have the upper body strength to do a lot more than I'm currently doing. I just need to check the shoulder, then practice the techniques myself to make sure it's safe." Arianne filled her glass with juice.

"Do you want us to come up to Spokane with you?" Pa helped himself to the toast and butter.

"I'm considering waiting to see if I can time it so that Lucy can come as well. She will have finished her nursing training by mid May. This trip might be something she could use to add to her experience."

"You get along well with Lucy. I'm glad," Gran said. "How are you getting along with Matthew now?"

Arianne took a bite of her toast, chewed, and chased it with a mouthful of apple juice. She could only avoid the question for so long before they noticed.

"We get along well as friends, but I've decided it's best if I pull back a bit. I don't want people getting the wrong idea."

"Wrong idea?" Pa raised his bushy eyebrows. "Do you think he might be interested in you?"

Arianne shook her head and held up her hand. "No. Just friends. But I don't want all the meddling Maggies to start applying pressure to either him or me."

Her answer seemed to satisfy her grandparents. It was a shame it wasn't completely true.

———

"I'd LOVE to come with you." Lucy's response was quick and enthusiastic when they spoke on the phone later that day. "If you can get an appointment and book into the program after commencement, that would be awesome. And you're right. Since knowing you, I've wanted to learn more about rehabilitation of people with spinal injuries."

"I'll let you know once I've got it arranged, and we'll see about booking accommodation."

"Wouldn't you stay in the hospital?" Lucy asked.

"It's a day class, so I'm free to go out on the town with you in the evening."

"Shame we couldn't get Matt to come as well." Lucy's comment provoked all kinds of ambiguous feelings. She wouldn't even tell Matt about it. It wouldn't be appropriate.

BUT THAT DIDN'T MEAN that Lucy wouldn't tell him.

"I heard you'll be going up to Spokane with Lucy." Matt said a week later, after they'd finished the exercise session.

"I'll be seeing a specialist about my shoulder." So Lucy had spoken to him. Was she glad about that?

"Yeah, you mentioned it last week. Are you worried?"

"About needing surgery?" Arianne was surprised by the look on his face. "I'm hopeful we're on the way to full strength and movement, so surgery won't be needed."

"I worry about you having surgery and having to go through rehabilitation again." Matt's eyes showed that he wasn't kidding.

"I'll do it if it means I can finally improve. I like the idea of being able to stand upright again. I wouldn't like the process, but it may be the only way."

He nodded and started shifting gym equipment into place.

"Matt?"

He looked up. "I'm just worried it might be worse for you."

What could be worse? Even as the thought went through her

mind, she rebuked herself. She'd met several people whose condition was worse than hers.

"By the way …" She swallowed the thought and changed the subject. "What do you think about me trying kayaking?"

"Funny you should say that." Matthew reached forward and did the lift transfer without even breaking conversation. "My brother, Caleb—the one who lives in Australia—told me about an Aussie movie, a true story about someone like you with an acquired injury, eventually learning to kayak and compete."

"True story? Really?"

"Yeah, I looked it up and streamed it. So inspiring."

"What was it called—the movie?"

"*Penguin Bloom.*"

"Crazy name for a movie."

"You wanna come over to our place and watch it with Lucy and the rest of the fam?"

Watch a movie with Matt? Her heart galloped off and took a lap around the building before he mentioned Lucy and the rest of the family. It returned home and sank.

"Sure. That sounds like fun."

"We can order pizza"

"Even better."

———

MID-MAY CAME AROUND QUICKLY. Arianne had secured an appointment with the specialist in Spokane, confirmed the transfer class, and booked accommodation for her and Lucy. She was looking forward to the possibilities.

And Matt had done some more research on how she could learn to kayak. Para canoeing had recently become an Olympic sport, and apparently there were slight modifications on para canoes to support floatation. They hadn't gone down to the lake yet, but Arianne was excited about the possibilities.

Even the discussion around healing had taken a different focus. Pa had been disappointed, of course. But Gran had continued to pray about the situation.

"You know, Ari," Gran said as they drank their morning coffee. "I've been watching some YouTube interviews with Joni Eareckson Tada and Nick Vujicic."

Arianne beamed and her heart warmed. That Gran even knew who those people were touched her deeply.

"First of all, that's very 'digital generation' of you to be watching YouTube, and second, they are both my go-to for inspiration. How did you find out about them?"

"Marianne Kennedy told me about them. Nick Vujicic is from Australia." Gran stood up from the table with her coffee cup in hand. "I can't believe how much God has used both of them in circumstances that would have floored the majority of us."

"There have been numerous quotes from both of them I'd like to have cross-stitched into a sampler and hung on the wall."

"If only you knew how to cross-stitch." Gran grinned in her direction.

"If only I knew someone who knew how to cross-stitch." Arianne grinned back. "If you're offering, I can give you my favorite."

"Which quote?"

"One of Joni's. 'When we honestly ask God the "why" question, He doesn't give us answers as much as He gives us Himself.'"

"I'll bet that has been a go-to quote in the last month."

Arianne sighed. "You have no idea.

"So what are you up to today?" Gran asked. "You're dressed for outdoors."

"I'm going to have a lesson in canoeing."

"What's that?" Pa called from the porch where he was kicking his yard boots off.

"Para canoeing. Like kayaking, but the boat is modified to aid balance for para-athletes."

"Is that safe?" Pa came into the kitchen and pulled a coffee cup out of the cupboard, filling it from the coffee pot.

"I'm not even going to answer that question." Arianne wheeled over to the kitchen counter, her coffee cup on her knee, which she placed into the dishwasher.

"We're just concerned, darlin'." Pa leaned against the counter and sipped his coffee.

"I know, but I thought we'd come to the place where you realized I'm a responsible adult. Now that I'm working so much with my occupational therapist, I've been aiming towards living an independent life. Do you honestly think I'm going to sign up for something that will make things worse for me?"

"But canoeing, honey? Really?" Gran asked, her voice raised.

"Para canoeing is an Olympic sport. And, for your information, I was inspired by a real-life para-athlete with a similar injury to mine. They made a movie about her."

"Well, if you've done the research, and you think you're capable, can we come watch?" Gran added her dishes to the dishwasher.

"I wish you would. Why don't you hire your own canoe? Then we can all have a nice time exercising on the lake."

"Lands sakes, Ari. A pair of oldies like us would likely sink the minute we pushed out from the edge."

"That's nonsense, Pa, and you know it. You're both quite capable. It would be fun to go on a family boating adventure."

"Were you going to go on your own?" Gran asked.

"No. Of course not. Lucy and Matt are picking me up, and we're going together."

"So you won't be paddling on your own."

"At this stage, the occupational therapist won't allow me to go on my own, but I will one day. You may be assured. That's the purpose of the whole exercise. I want to get back to competing in something, and this seems like a reasonable opportunity to investigate."

Gran shrugged and raised her eyebrows in Pa's direction. "What do you say, Pa?"

"Sounds like you've done your research. Why don't you go and test the waters, so to speak. If you think it's going to work out, we'll come with you next time." Pa went to his recliner and picked up the newspaper.

"No fear, Jolly Rayne." Gran snatched the paper out of his hand. "If Arianne is going to try a new adventure, then so are we."

Pa groaned and pulled himself out of his chair. "If we capsize and sink to the bottom of the lake, don't say I didn't warn you."

"He means us, Ari." Gran turned to pull sandwich fixings from the refrigerator. "I have every confidence that you will do very well on the water."

Arianne looked towards Pa, who shrugged and huffed. He had doubts. If she was honest, she had a few doubts as well, but she was going to try. Hannah Gilbertson had loved the idea of having a modified canoe to offer for those who needed the extra stability, and she'd let Arianne know it had arrived. Today was the trial day for everyone—Hannah, as the owner of the rowing club, Matt as the self-appointed coach, and Arianne as the operator.

———

"So you're sure about this?" Lucy fired the question as Matthew pulled his truck up out front of the Raynes' place.

"The point is, Ari is sure about it. We're just here to support her." He honked the horn, then got out of the driver's side.

"Classy." Lucy got out of the passenger side.

"What do you mean, classy?"

"Honking for your girlfriend to come out. What happened to knocking on the front door?"

"You're ridiculous. You know Ari and I have agreed that we're just friends."

"Sure." Lucy had a sing-song tone much like a grade schooler set on tease.

Matthew opened the garden gate and started up the path, but Arianne was already on the porch and wheeling down the side access ramp, her grandparents following.

"Do you mind if Gran and Pa come along for the afternoon?" Arianne called as she wheeled up to him.

The older couple were dressed for the outdoors, and Jolly Rayne carried a backpack that looked like it was bulging with supplies.

"The more the merrier, I guess," Matthew said. "It's your show."

"Show?" Arianne wheeled through the gate and pulled up next to Matthew's truck.

"Your trial on the water."

"I hope you're not all going to stand on the lakefront and watch me."

"It's tempting." Matthew put his arms around her to lift her to standing height before scooping her up into the truck.

"Don't listen to him," Lucy clambered into the center seat from the driver's side. "He might stand and gawk, but I'm looking forward to an afternoon on the water."

"Apart from anything else, the OT won't allow me on the water on my own until it's all been tested and proved safe."

Matthew turned to put Arianne's chair in the back of the truck, but Jolly Rayne beat him to it, hoisting it over the side.

"Sorry there isn't room for you in my truck. Will you follow us to the rowing club?"

"We're all set, son." Jolly and Ruth went to their vehicle. Matthew felt a bit strange. They could have brought their granddaughter to the lake. This felt a bit like a date, despite the fact he had his sister and Ari's grandparents along for the ride.

"I can't wait for our trip to Spokane." Lucy spoke to Arianne as Matthew got behind the wheel. "Are you excited?"

"Excited isn't really the right word for it," Arianne said. "More like anxious."

"Anxious?" Matthew felt a lump of something cold in his gut. "Why?"

"I don't know." Arianne shrugged. "I've had such a lot of trouble with this shoulder, I'm hoping it won't seize up just when I'm finally going to learn the transfers."

"Your strength has improved," Matthew said.

"I know." Arianne sighed.

"What?" Matthew was glad Lucy asked.

"I'll be seeing the specialist to talk about if I'll be strong enough to start learning to walk."

Matthew changed gears as he left the Rayne property, building up speed onto the main road into town. He wasn't sure what to say.

"Sorry, Ari." Lucy sounded genuinely chagrined. "I was thinking more about us spending time together and enjoying some city nightlife."

"I don't plan on dancing, if that's what you mean."

Matthew glanced at Arianne's expression. She was smiling. He felt relieved that she seemed to be joking with Lucy.

"Do you think you'll have this transfer using a slide board perfected by the time you get back?" Matthew changed the subject.

"I hope so. You must be getting tired of having to pick me up all the time."

"Yeah, it's a real chore, right Matt?" Lucy waggled her eyebrows at him. Her insinuation was very close to the truth. There was no chore about it. Once Arianne began to transfer on her own—at the gym, into her own vehicle—he would be surplus to requirements. And apart from being needed, he would be losing the opportunity to be physically close. That wasn't such a nice thought.

"Pa has been negotiating with a car yard in Walla Walla on a small hatchback." Arianne either didn't pick up Lucy's meaning, or she was ignoring it. "Once we sign on it, we can take it to a specialist workshop to have the braking and gas modifications installed."

"Oh, wow. It won't be long and you won't need us at all." Lucy's words hit Matthew like a brick.

"Of course I'll need you. A girl's gotta have friends, right? I hope you two aren't going to just disappear into the background once I can get around on my own."

Lucy grabbed Arianne's hand and gushed in some sort of friends-forever sentiment, but all Matthew could feel was urgency. He had to decide. If Ari was ready to take the next step in rehabilitation—literally—he couldn't come to her with his heart then. Even he knew that he had to commit to her now, come what may—for better or for worse—or not at all. Delaying his decision until later would seem like he'd waited to see how things would turn out.

Like Gavin.

Ari and Lucy were leaving for Spokane in a few days.

It was time to make a decision.

———

"You've paddled a canoe before, I assume?" The owner of the rowing club, Hannah Gilbertson, seemed to be checking off a list.

"I used to go to summer camp here when I was a kid. I've done a few laps around Lake Other in my time." Arianne used her arms to get comfortable in the canoe seat.

"It should be fine with me in the boat, shouldn't it?" Lucy

directed her question toward the OT who'd come down to this first-time-on-water exercise.

The occupational therapist, who Adam Lancaster had arranged for Arianne, had already helped Ari position herself, checking support and stability. She nodded in Lucy's direction.

"I'll keep the Jet Ski handy in case you capsize. You can swim, can't you?" Hannah seemed concerned, despite Ari's life jacket and helmet.

"Not sure I can swim to shore, but I can stay afloat. I'll be fine. I'd feel better if you were more worried about my grandparents."

"Don't you worry about us," Pa called over. He had his life jacket on and was sizing up one of the canoes. "We were brought up on these here lakes."

Arianne smiled. She hadn't been on an outdoor activity with her grandparents in years. This was such a good idea, and the weather was perfect.

Hannah stepped back and surveyed the rest of the group, leaving Arianne and Lucy floating in shallow water at the lake's edge. Matt dragged a canoe over and put it into the water next to Arianne. "You'll let me know if you feel unsafe, right?" he said.

Arianne resisted the urge to roll her eyes. "I'm going to be fine, Matt. Even if I get swamped by a freak wave—which I won't, since we're on an inland lake—I know how to stay afloat." She tapped her life jacket to emphasize her words. "But I would appreciate it if you would shove us into the water."

Matthew smiled and moved to the back of the boat. He had such a cute smile. Such a waste on someone who was just a friend.

"You okay?" Matt called as Arianne's canoe floated.

"We're fine." Lucy called.

"Yes, I'm fine." Arianne used all her self-control to keep her voice light and breezy, clamping down the annoyance. She wanted to do this and believed she could, especially with Lucy on board.

"Ready?" She spoke to Lucy who was in front of her.

"Ready. Do you want to call the rhythm?"

"Sure." Even as Arianne gripped the paddle and, in unison with Lucy, propelled them into deeper water, she felt the joy of strength. All those weights and exercises meant she was in good condition for paddling. Her right shoulder was so much stronger than it had been several months ago.

Fifteen yards from shore she spoke to Lucy. "Let's turn and see how the others are progressing."

Lucy cooperated, turning slightly to give a view of the shore.

"What's wrong?" Pa called from his canoe the moment they began to turn. He and Gran were nearest to them in the water.

"Nothing's wrong. In fact, nothing could be better." The words had hardly left her mouth when Arianne saw Matt, still on shore, in the grips of Heidi. The image of Ursula from *The Little Mermaid* came to mind, and she wanted to laugh, but didn't. Firstly because it was an unkind thought, and secondly, jealousy had leaped out at her like a jack-in-the-box and was springing all kinds of insecurity in her direction. What was she doing?

"How are you finding it?" Gran and Pa approached, each of them apparently confident, Gran asking the question.

"It's great. What about you?" Arianne clamped down the unwanted feelings of jealousy at the sight of Matt with Heidi. "Let's head out further," she said to Lucy, and turned their canoe out toward the deep.

"Can't say as I've paddled in a long while," Gran said. "I'm not sure I'm as fit as you, with all your weekly exercises."

"So would now be a good time to challenge you to a race?" Arianne laughed with her grandparents.

"You don't think I'd let you win that easily, do you?" Pa put extra force into his stroke to pull ahead.

"Perhaps you should calm down." Gran called. "We need to make sure it's all safe."

"It's safe," Arianne said. "I feel remarkably balanced. You feel balanced, don't you Luce?"

"At the moment." Lucy was paddling in swift, strong strokes, which Arianne matched.

As they paddled, Arianne enjoyed the therapeutic feel of the canoe slicing through the water, the warmth of the late spring sunshine and the joy of freedom. It was almost perfect—except she couldn't ignore the glimpses of Matt in conversation with Heidi, and the tentacle-like hold she had on him. And he didn't seem to be putting any effort into resisting her. Fudge. Their canoe drew away from shore. She didn't want to see it. Of course Matthew was going to respond to a beautiful woman flirting with him. Why shouldn't he? The relationship he had with her was just friends.

"Come on, Lucy. Let's race."

CHAPTER FOURTEEN

"Matthew Kennedy. I'm so glad to see you. This is perfect." Heidi's nasally voice sounded from behind.

Matthew's attention was drawn from his almost mother-hen like focus on Arianne.

"It's so good to see you." Before he'd had a chance to redirect his thoughts, she'd stepped up and kissed him—not on the cheek, which would have been bad enough, but on the lips.

The urge to wipe his mouth clean was overwhelming, but Heidi had her arm around his waist and was already getting her phone camera ready.

"It's been ages since I've seen you, and my followers have been begging me to catch up with you again."

"Ah ... I'm just here with ..." Matthew looked out to the water. Arianne, her grandparents, and his sister were paddling confidently.

"Just a couple of minutes, Matthew. Your family won't mind."

Heidi obviously recognized Lucy. Did she recognize Arianne? Did he want to mention that he was here with Ari and her family? Like a date, except it wasn't a date, and they were just friends. At the moment. Nope. Too complicated.

"I'm not really comfortable with your online exposure. Remember, I kind of said that a while ago?"

"Kind of? You were rather rude about it, actually, but I'll forgive you. Hey, peeps." She turned her camera on and focused the phone in his direction. He wanted to wriggle out of her grip but didn't want to embarrass her. "Look who I found out at the local rowing club. Say hi, babes."

"Hi." Matthew wanted to tell them to get a life, to leave him alone, that he was on an important date, but he wasn't like Heidi who could just talk in front of camera. The opposite. If anything, he became tongue-tied.

"He's looking cute, isn't he, girls?" Heidi stood back and allowed the camera to take in her smoothing her hands over his arms, clearly visible in his t-shirt. Matthew's muscles tightened, especially in his gut. He needed to take control.

"Hey, Heidi and online fans, just a heads-up. I'm actually here on a date, so hope you don't mind if I leave you to it." He pulled himself away and moved toward his canoe, but he couldn't close his ears.

"A date? Well that's terrible news for us, hey girls? Who's the lucky woman?"

"Not today, Heidi. Sorry. Have a great day."

As he shouldered into his life vest, he heard shouting out in the water. He looked up and the blood in his veins turned to ice. Why was Arianne's canoe so far out and what was floating in the water?

"Is that wheelchair girl?" Heidi had sidled next to him again and was following his gaze. Matthew gritted his teeth. He didn't want to be rude, but so help him …

"Is she your date?" The scorn was practically dripping from her lips. "Come on, babes. You can do better than that."

Matthew turned on Heidi, struggling to keep his emerging

anger in check.

"What?" She took a step back and held up her fake-nail bedecked hands in a stop, surrender pose. "You're not serious. Surely. What sort of life would you have with someone like her?"

"Honestly, Heidi, I don't know, but I'm up for the challenge. That's what happens when you love someone."

"Love? Whoa. This is serious. Wait 'til my peeps hear about this."

"Stop, Heidi! You don't own me, nor do you have rights to discuss me or anyone related to me on a public forum. So just don't."

"It's a free country, babes. You're a hot topic."

"In your world, maybe, but in the real world, I'm an ordinary guy who's trying to have an ordinary life. Can you just leave it. Please."

"Whatever." Heidi turned back to her phone, which he hoped had been momentarily paused. "Totes awks, peeps. Our boy Matthew is taken, so he tells me. Such a shame." She turned back and called to Matthew. "You should see the feed exploding, Matthew. Never too late to reconsider."

Thankfully, Heidi walked away. Reconsider? He had been doing nothing but consider—for the first time—and now he'd had this "totes awks" interaction with Heidi the influencer, who had drawn a confession out of him. Did he really love Arianne? Well, whatever it was he felt strongly about her and wanted to be with her. Love? Possibly. The beginnings, at least. But he hadn't given Arianne any indication of what had been going on in his heart. Didn't even know if she was interested in him. It wasn't necessarily a given, after his disastrous start. He hoped that Arianne didn't follow Heidi's World. He needed to say something to her first.

―――

THIS FELT SO GOOD, the speed they'd been able to generate, paddling through the water.

"Keep up!" She was aware that they'd outpaced her grand-parents, by the quick glance over her shoulder. But she wasn't going to do that—look backward—too often. It had seemed like a natural thing to do until she remembered the muscles she should have used for balance in her thighs and butt were not engaged. For those fifteen wonderful minutes of exercise, she had forgotten she was a person with a disability.

Eyes forward, she saw another boat on the water, a small motorboat that had come to a stop. A man stood and threw a large black trash bag into the water, then started the motor and sped off.

"What's he doing?" Lucy asked.

"Hey! Don't throw your trash in the lake!" It was pointless yelling. He probably couldn't hear over the sound of the outboard motor. "Just because you're irresponsible, doesn't mean I'm going to leave your plastic to pollute the lake."

"What a loser," Lucy said. Obviously she was of the same mind as Arianne as she worked in unison to direct their canoe toward the floating bag of trash. But the closer they got, the more alarmed Arianne became. The bag hadn't sunk much. There must be air trapped inside. But the sound of yipping caused Arianne's muscles to engage and move even faster.

"What are you doing?" Lucy asked.

"Hurry up, Luce. I think there are puppies in the bag."

They were able to draw up near the bag as it was beginning to sink. They weren't quite close enough to reach it, but Arianne forgot all caution at the sound of what must be puppies.

"Come on." She was closer to the bag than Lucy, straining as she reached her paddle out to try and draw the bag closer.

"Wait." Lucy was trying to paddle them closer, but the bag was nearly under water, and Arianne ignored her.

As she stretched out further, she could feel the canoe tilting.

She should try to balance, especially since Lucy was shouting at her, but as she'd found before, her lower muscles were absent without leave, and she no longer had the ability to right herself. They were going to capsize.

She could swim. She hoped. But she was not going to let those puppies drown. She stopped fighting the tilt and allowed herself to go into the water. The canoe capsized. Now was the test. In the pool, she had float devices to support her legs. Here she had the life jacket to aid, and her own upper strength to move through the water and grab the bag.

"Help, Lucy! Quickly!"

"Let the bag go!" Lucy was only a couple of yards away. "I'll get it."

"I can't." Arianne lifted the bag. "It will sink, and we'll lose them."

"Are you all right?" Pa's voice indicated he wasn't far away.

"Here. Luce. Grab the bag."

It was difficult keeping the bag and herself afloat. But she wasn't going to let the puppies drown.

"Just let the bag go, Ari," Lucy swam closer.

"That man was trying to drown puppies." Arianne held the bag as high out of the water as she could. "Here. Take them. Hurry up, please."

Thankfully, Lucy stopped arguing, and hefted the bag of whimpering wiggling puppies—at least, Ari assumed they were puppies—as high out of the water as she could, scissor kicking her way over to their capsized canoe. Now, with two arms free, Arianne propelled herself to join Lucy, hanging onto the canoe.

"You could have died." Lucy complained.

"Did you want me to let them drown?" Arianne had a good grip on her canoe and was able to conduct the conversation without much trouble.

"Lands sakes, Ari!" Pa and Gran paddled up close. "What on earth were you doing?"

"Rescuing animals. And I don't need a lecture. I'm fine."

"You're stuck in the water, is what you are." Pa paddled close. "Do you think I can hoist you into my boat without tipping us both in the water?"

"Take the puppies first." Arianne gestured toward the black bag.

"What on earth …?" Gran was close enough to take the bag from Lucy. By the wriggling and crying coming from inside, Arianne was certain the man had been trying to drown puppies. Gran opened the bag revealing two shivering doe-eyed black pups.

"Ooh. The poor little things." Arianne switched her hold to her grandparents' canoe.

"Never mind about the dogs," Pa said. "You're in the water and could have drowned."

"I'm not going to drown," Arianne said. "You're not going to drown, are you, Luce?"

Lucy shook her head with a resigned smile.

"Our boat's a bit crowded, but we might be able to get you aboard," Pa said.

"It's worth a try, I guess. But I don't want to land you in the water. Then there'd be four of us to rescue."

Pa reached out his strong arm, muscled from years of farm labor. Arianne gripped his forearm and he gripped hers, but though he raised her, the canoe was too unsteady for him to drag her in.

"I don't want to tip you over, Pa."

"Hannah's coming on the Jet Ski." Lucy pointed in the direction of the rowing club.

But it wasn't Hannah who pulled up next to them. It was Matt, and his face was pale, a picture of panic.

"Ari, are you all right?" Matt's breath was accelerated as well.

"I'm fine."

"I couldn't see you behind the canoe. I thought …"

"I'm fine, Matt. Honestly, I'm fine. Let's see if you can hoist me on behind you."

"Were you worried about me, brother dear?" Lucy asked, still holding the overturned canoe."

Matt ignored his sister.

"It might be easier if you grab hold of the rescue sled, and I'll tow you back to shore."

"Do you think you can rescue Lucy as well?" Arianne smiled in his direction.

"Sure. Maybe one at a time."

Arianne moved hand over hand along Pa's canoe to move to a point where she could grasp Matt's hand. She then used the same process to reach the rescue sled towed behind the Jet Ski. Taking hold of the hand grips, she lay stomach down on the board.

"Are those puppies all right?" She looked over to Gran, who had the black trash bag open.

"I'll take care of the puppies," Gran called. "You get back on shore safely."

"Puppies?" Matt turned a questioning eye in her direction.

"Never mind. Let's get back to shore, so I can get back on the horse."

Matt didn't make any comment about her horse metaphor, just used the throttle to move the Jet Ski gently through the water. If they thought she was done, they had another think coming. Canoeing was going to become a regular activity in her life. And possibly puppy rescue.

———

MATTHEW'S HEAD was all over the place. Ruth Rayne had a black trash bag with two wriggling, wet, and whimpering pups, and she placed it in the cab of his truck. His suggestion that they take the puppies to the Junk Man to look after was summarily dismissed. To make matters worse, Arianne had insisted she was going to go canoeing again, though she had conceded she needed to call it quits for today. Instead of him having been her coach and guardian for the day, he'd been distracted and unavailable when she needed him. Now her grandfather had taken matters in hand, and they were getting ready to take Arianne home. Not what he wanted. He needed to talk to her.

"When are you guys leaving for Spokane?" Matthew asked Lucy.

"Tomorrow. Why?"

"I need to talk to Ari for a few minutes."

"Don't start lecturing her about rescuing the pups. I couldn't have let them drown either."

"But you have the use of all your limbs. It's slightly different."

"Matthew." There was warning in Lucy's tone. "She doesn't need a lecture."

Lecture? That was the last thing on his mind. He needed to tell her how he felt. Heidi Glasson and all her fake fans knew, and he was dead scared Ari might have started following Heidi just to see what she was up to.

"I won't be long. You'd better try to figure out what we're going to do with those dogs, since you won't take them over to Brandon Taylor's dad. You know his reputation is caring for distressed animals. It would be the easiest thing to do."

"I'll keep the Junk Man in mind, but at this stage, we're going to keep them, of course."

Matthew didn't bother to argue with Lucy's throw away comment. It wasn't going to be his responsibility. Instead, he walked across to the Raynes' SUV.

"Could I talk to you for a moment?" Matthew asked Arianne, who was waiting next to the front passenger door.

"Sure." Arianne released the brakes and wheeled closer to him.

"I ... ah ... I wondered if I could talk to you for a bit."

"Yes. You've already said that."

"Are you ready, darlin'?" Pa had finished putting their picnic gear in the back of the car and came over.

"Won't be a moment," Arianne replied. "Just talking to Matt."

Matthew swallowed. He hadn't thought about what to say. His heart knew what he wanted to share, but his brain couldn't form a sensible way to say the words, and Ari's grandparents were waiting only a few yards away.

"I just wanted you to know that … well … when I saw you'd gone in the water today, I panicked. I care about you, Ari."

"Thanks, Matt. I care about you too, as good friends do. Thanks for helping with the rescue."

Good friends? He'd botched that one. That wasn't what he'd meant.

"It's okay, Matt. I understand." Ari reached out and squeezed his hand. "You're a good friend."

She let go of his hand and turned her chair back towards the car.

"Do you want to go out later—to talk about the puppies?" Where had that invitation come from? But it was the best he could come up with under pressure.

"I'd better not—I've got to get ready for the trip tomorrow. But I will call Lucy about them. We'll have to do something responsible, now we've rescued them."

"Okay. I'll be praying for you the whole time you're away." That was so not what Matthew wanted to say. What he needed to say. But Arianne couldn't read his mind. Or perhaps she could, and she was trying to avoid an awkward moment. He let her go and watched jealously as Jolly Rayne lifted his granddaughter into his car.

He wanted to do the lifting, and holding, and kissing. Yep. It was true. He knew it for certain. For better or for worse, he wanted Arianne Rayne in his life, no matter what.

CHAPTER FIFTEEN

The specialist had given the go-ahead for Arianne to begin a new program. Her hard work on the physical therapy exercises had done wonders with her shoulder, and strength was returning—at last. And the work in the pool had been designed to target specific neural pathways. With this new program, neuroplasticity would likely cause new pathways to develop to support leg movement. All of this was good news.

"Successful trip?" Matt asked the question when he picked them up from the bus station.

"Very." Arianne had so much to tell, she didn't know where to start.

"You should see her in action." Lucy sat in her usual position, right between them in the front of Matt's truck.

"I should have let you use the slide board to get in the truck on your own." Matt had got them on the road out towards the farm.

"I feel confident using it, but I wouldn't for the truck. It's too high up."

"Right."

"Sorry. If you don't mind, you'll still have to assist on occasion," Arianne said.

"It's my pleasure."

Arianne glanced his way. He was being weird, and she couldn't figure out why.

"How are the puppies?" she asked.

"They're still together. Your gran has both of them. She thought it best they have each other until you two got home."

Arianne laughed. "She wasn't so keen on me deciding to keep one. I'm glad she didn't get rid of them while I was away."

"Mom wasn't that keen on me keeping one either," Lucy said.

"I plan to train mine to be a companion dog." Arianne had done some research and thought it couldn't be too hard.

"Aren't companion dogs bred specifically? They have specialized training as well." What was that note of doubt in Matt's tone?

"Well, I mean to give it a try." Arianne was determined to not let anyone derail her from engaging with life to the full. "What have you been up to while we've been away?" She turned her best smile in Matt's direction.

"Just work. Nothing special."

He sure was full of enthusiasm today.

"How's your girlfriend?" Lucy asked.

Matt jerked his gaze toward his sister for a second. "What?"

"Eyes on the road." Arianne had her usual moment of anxiety.

"What are you talking about?" Matt turned his attention back on the drive.

"Heidi's World tells us you're taken," Lucy said. "Thought you might like to fill us in, since I'm your sister, and Arianne is a good friend."

Arianne didn't actually want to know. She'd been hoping it was just another one of Heidi's plays for attention.

"Can we ask for a name?" Lucy was ruthless.

"No. You can't. I'll tell you when I'm good and ready."

"So there is someone?"

"Lucy." Arianne felt Matt's unwillingness to share, and it was awkward. Especially since she was totally jealous of the unnamed girlfriend.

"Oh, fine." Lucy gave a fake pout. "Anyway, Arianne has loads to tell, so …" Lucy waved her hand in Arianne's direction, as if to cue her.

"I'm going back in early August to begin working on a new program. By October, I plan to work with my PT to get some new muscles moving. If all goes well, I might be able to stand upright by Christmas."

"Walk? You'll be able to walk?" Matt had a frown on his face and in his tone.

"Maybe. With walking aids, if all goes to plan."

"That's awesome news, isn't it, Matt?" Lucy glared at her brother.

"Of course it's awesome."

"What's got your goat today? You're acting strange." Lucy asked the question at the front of Arianne's mind.

"Nothing. It's great news, Ari. I'm pleased for you."

"Yes, well, I'll be haunting the gym at all hours. I hope you're still going to help train me."

"Of course."

"And Jeannette has offered me some work as well. She wants me to do some courses in personal training."

"She mentioned it to me."

"You don't sound pleased." Lucy always asked what Arianne was thinking but was too sensitive to ask.

"I'm pleased. Of course I'm pleased. Cut it out, Luce."

"Right, well here we are, home sweet home." Arianne made the comment and meant it. Of all the places she'd ever lived with her parents—and there'd been plenty—this was the one place she felt as if it were home. "Thanks for the lift, Matt."

"Sure." He got out of the truck and had her wheelchair waiting by the time she had her legs facing out.

"Too high for me to work on my own." She smiled at him, and though he reached his arms out to lift her down, there was something troubling him. She wished she knew what.

Did he really have a girlfriend? In Heidi's words, that would be totes awks.

———

"What's wrong?" Lucy asked the question the moment they were back in the truck after seeing Arianne inside. She had one of the puppies on her knee.

"Nothing."

"Something. Matt, have you got a girlfriend?" Lucy scratched the puppy behind its ear.

"Arianne."

"Arianne is in the house."

Matthew didn't say anything. Couldn't Lucy guess? Did he have to spell it out? A few miles passed before Lucy spoke again.

"Do you mean Arianne? Like, Arianne is your girlfriend?"

Matthew nodded.

"Did you just say that to get Heidi off your back?"

"What? No. I didn't mean to tell Heidi anything. She just guessed."

"But you haven't asked Arianne."

"I know."

"Why?"

"I wanted to. I tried after the incident at the lake."

"What did you say?"

"Not much. I told her I cared about her—like the accident scared the daylights out of me."

"And?"

"I told her I cared about her."

"And what did she say?"

"That she knew, and that's what good friends do."

"She thinks you're just friends." Lucy flopped back against the seat.

"I know."

"Perhaps that's all she wants. Perhaps she isn't interested in you."

"That's what I'm scared of."

"Bro. You have to talk to her—properly."

"I tried to organize a proper talk, away from you and the grandparents, but she had to pack to go away."

"And now we're back. Are you going to try again?"

"I better, I guess. I'm not in a great state of mind not knowing."

"I could tell."

Lucy fell silent, leaving Matthew to his own thoughts. Had he left it too late? Would she think he was only asking because of her news? That was why he'd tried to talk to her before she saw the specialist, so she'd know he meant it, come what may.

When they arrived home, Lucy bounded inside with her new puppy, leaving him to bring her luggage. He didn't mind. He needed the extra time with his thoughts. Wait.

"Lucy?" He sought her attention after he'd put her bag in her room.

"Yeah?" She had the puppy and was scrunching an old blanket into a cardboard box.

"Does Ari think Heidi is my girlfriend?"

Lucy stood upright and looked at him, a puzzled expression on her face. "Heidi?"

"Yeah. She was at the lakeshore the day you found the puppies, and she was all over me like sunscreen."

"Do you think Ari saw?"

"Maybe. Did she say anything to you?"

"Ari was the one who looked up Heidi's World and saw all the fallout from the announcement."

"She thinks I have the hots for Heidi."

"Bro. You're hopeless at communication. Remember Jane?"

"I'd appreciate it if you wouldn't remind me of past romantic disasters."

"But you have to learn from your mistakes. You have to communicate properly, not beat around the bush."

Matthew groaned inwardly. He'd never been as quick as his siblings in talking on the fly. He was more a sit-and-think-about-it-for-an-hour type of guy. That was evident any time Heidi Glasson thrust a camera in his face. If her online fans had any idea what he really thought, they'd drop him like a hot rock. But he wanted Arianne to know what he really thought, and trying to talk to her with overbearing relatives hovering around was a silly idea. He needed to spend some time alone with her. And not at the gym.

"By the look on your face, I'd say you're hatching a plan." Lucy put down two plastic containers, one with water and one with puppy food. "Do you need any help?"

"For once in my life, I need to figure this one out on my own. But thanks."

"No probs. I'm going to go with Dad to the Walla Walla Airport shortly to pick up Mia."

"Is Mia coming home?"

"That she is, bro. You don't keep close tabs on the fam, do you?"

"I keep tabs on you."

"That's probably because I'm Arianne's close friend."

"Maybe. How long is Mia home for?"

"The entire summer. She's been away in LA for so long I've almost forgotten what she looks like."

"So I guess the whole crowd will be around for dinner soon?"

"I guess. Ask Mom."

This was important to find out if there was going to be a family dinner, because he needed to make sure nothing would clash with his making a date. It might take him a long time to get around to something, but once he'd made up his mind, he didn't want anything interfering with his plans.

———

"It's so good to have you home, darlin'." Pa kissed Arianne on the head as he came past.

Arianne smiled as she stroked her puppy behind the ear. "It's good to be home."

"So you feel confident this new rehabilitation program is going to work?" Gran peeled potatoes at the kitchen counter as they talked.

"The specialist said we have a strong chance of success and seemed positive about the likelihood of learning to walk again."

"Seems like God has been answering our prayers after all." Pa sat on the couch next to Arianne.

"I've been thanking God daily, ever since the healing meeting, but this new development is a further answer. I mean, I know that I won't be running or anything crazy. I'll need walking aids. But even being upright again will be a huge improvement."

"That's great, Ari. What have your parents had to say about it?" Gran put the saucepan of potatoes on the stove.

"You know Mom. She's always got a reason to find something negative to say."

"But she's pleased, surely?" Pa reached for the puppy and cuddled him to his chest when Arianne released him.

"She's pleased in her own way. Anyway, what I want to know is when are we going to try out my new car?"

"We can go for a spin up the drive now, if you want to show me what you can do."

"Don't you be going out for too long. Dinner is only half an hour away." Gran had to talk loudly over the spit and crackle of boiling oil as she put some coated chicken in to fry.

"I only want to practice getting in and seeing if I can make it work. We'll be twenty minutes, tops."

"See that you are. I'm only letting you off from helping with dinner because it's your first night home."

Ari took the pup back from Pa and placed him in his little dog basket.

"What are you going to call that critter?" Pa asked. "We can't keep calling him 'pup.'"

"I'd have thought you would have named him while I was gone." Arianne rolled to the door.

"I was leaving it up to you. I wasn't even sure which dog you'd choose." Pa opened the front door.

"I'll think on it." She rolled out onto the porch and down the access ramp, following Pa as he crossed the yard to the small yellow hatchback that was parked under the tree.

"You got your slide board?" He tossed the keys to her.

Arianne took a deep breath. It was time to see how much she'd gained in confidence. She pressed the remote fob to unlock the car. Pa went across to open the door.

"Wait. Let me see if I can do it on my own." She rolled over and Pa stepped back. Reaching out she opened the door and maneuvered herself to a park at a forty-five degree angle facing the door, as close as she could get. Locking the brakes, she detached the footrests and threw them on the ground.

"Usually I'd throw them on the passenger seat, but you'll have to sit there, won't you?" She grinned at Pa. Reaching over her shoulder, she retrieved the slide board from the bag on the back of her chair. After tilting the car side armrest back, she inserted the slide board underneath her right hip and

166

made sure it was resting securely against the back of the car seat.

"Right. Here it goes. Are you watching?"

"Like a hawk." And he was—hovering nearby, tensed as if he expected her to fall.

"Relax, Pa. I can do this." Arianne used her left arm to push and grabbed the inside fold-down roof handle with her right hand to pull herself onto and along the board. Two more moves, this time using the steering wheel, and she landed on the driver's seat. Reaching down, she lifted her right leg then her left, and she was seated ready to drive.

"What about your chair?" Pa asked.

"That's for another time. I'll need a new chair that I can dismantle and lift in pieces. For today, I'm going to leave it here for our return." She clicked her seatbelt in place, leaned out to move the chair away, then pulled the door closed.

Pa came around to the passenger side and got in. "That was impressive, darlin'."

"What will be impressive is if I can make this new-fangled thing work. I assume you've tried it already?"

"Nothing could be easier."

And it was remarkably easy. Pushing one lever forward engaged the brakes. A side button for acceleration. Only a few jerky movements before Arianne was able to control the car and drive all the way to the main road and back.

"How does it feel?" Pa asked.

"Like freedom. Though I'll have to have the OT do a thorough check and do another test for my license."

"Plenty of time for that. Let's get back for some of Gran's fried chicken."

Arianne drove near where she'd left her chair and began the process in reverse. She'd only just got the chair correctly placed when her phone rang.

"I'll only be a minute." She smiled at Pa. Looking at her

phone, she felt a jolt of something silly in her stomach. Matthew Kennedy.

"Hi, Matt."

"Hey. Are you busy?"

"Depends on how you look at it."

Matt didn't answer.

"I'm right in the middle of getting myself out of my new car and back into my wheelchair. What's up?"

A beat of silence.

"Matt?"

"Uh. You tried your new car?"

"Yes. It was great. I can't wait to drive you around for a change."

More strange silence.

"Matt, what's up? You're very quiet."

"I ... ah ... do you want to go on a date?"

CHAPTER SIXTEEN

A date. It was done. He'd actually asked Arianne on a date and she'd said yes and now his stomach was twisting itself into knots as he made plans. Where should they go?

Cafe? Too many people.

Restaurant in Walla Walla? Too much, too soon.

A picnic? The idea had possibilities, but there were so many things to arrange.

"Why don't you ask Mom to pack you a hamper?" Lucy asked during one of his brainstorming sessions with her.

"No. If I'm going to bring something from home, don't you think I should put it together myself? I need to make an effort. Now she's said yes, I need her to know that I mean business."

"You're not going to propose, bro. It's too soon for that."

Matthew frowned at her. A proposal was the end goal, but Lucy was right. It was way too soon for that.

"She needs to find out if a relationship with you is something she wants."

"You're right. But I still want to get something nice."

"Ask Leah Thompson. She does picnic hampers from her health food store."

"Good idea. And I could pick some dessert and coffee up from Becky. She has some good stuff, right?"

The idea began to take shape in his mind. They'd planned for late on Friday afternoon. The weather was forecast to be warm, and sunset wasn't until after nine.

Friday approached at a snail's pace. He'd asked Jeanette if he could leave early so he could pick up the hamper before Leah closed for the day. Just as he was getting in his truck, the phone rang.

Caleb.

"Hey, bro. What time is it there?"

"Morning. I'm just getting ready for work but wanted to catch you before I left. It'll be too late to call you when I get home."

"Good to hear from you. How is everybody?"

"By everybody, if you mean Alanah, she's good."

"All going well. Anything to report?"

"That's why I'm calling."

Matthew had a split second of anxiety. Given his brother rarely called, he hoped nothing was wrong.

"We've set a date."

The worry evaporated and happiness filled its place.

"You're getting married?"

"That's usually what happens when you've been engaged for a while. We just needed to sort some things out, and now it's done. January seventh. I'm hoping the whole fam will come."

"You're getting married Down Under?"

"Well, yeah. All of Alanah's family are here. One lot of relatives are going to have to travel. Seeing as I live here now, I thought the Kennedy clan could make a trip back to the old place."

Matthew had a flash of memories from his teenage years and his five years at the Australian high school. He'd been sixteen when the family moved back to the States, and he hadn't returned to Australia since.

"Have you asked Mum and Dad?" Just thinking about Australia, Matthew reverted to the Aussie pronunciation.

"I called them just before. I'll call Sasha and Derek next. Mum said she'd tell Lucy and Mia."

"Well, I better keep my focus on saving if I'm going to come up with airfares by January."

"Don't worry about accommodation. Alanah's family and some of the church people will help billet everyone out."

"That's awesome, bro."

"What about you? Mum said you've got a love interest."

"I'm working on it. Getting ready for a date as we speak."

"Let me know how it goes. If you're serious and want her to come as well, I'll make arrangements for accommodation."

Matthew disconnected the call. He was so happy for his brother, but the question had knocked him. He was serious about Arianne. Very serious, but could she travel internationally? Something to consider. But first, he needed to get this food hamper sorted.

———

Now she'd been passed to drive, Arianne decided to drive into town to meet Matt. Pa came with her. He was going to take her car back home, and besides, she was still gaining confidence about driving. The support was helpful at this stage.

They had agreed to meet in the parking lot near Becky's Coffee Cart. It was a good job she was so focused on driving, as it diverted her thoughts from the swarming butterflies threatening to break loose and make her dizzy.

"You want me to come back and pick you up?" Pa asked as he positioned her wheelchair near the door.

Arianne saw Matt was already there, and he was approaching. She hadn't discussed it with him, but she hoped Matt would take her home. She hoped ... she hoped a lot of things, but hope was one of those things she'd learned to be cautious about.

"I'll call you if I need you." Arianne placed her slide board in place, ready to exit.

"Hey, Ari." She looked up as Matt approached. He smiled, and her heart melted into a warm puddle.

"Hey. Look what I can do." She smiled back while doing the moves that landed her in her wheelchair. Pa handed her the footrests, and she was ready to roll.

"Wow." Matt shook Pa's hand, since they were standing practically on top of each other. Two hovering men, and she'd still managed to transfer mostly unaided.

"So you'll call me?" Pa got into the driver's seat, once Arianne had moved away.

"If I need to." She was going to have to have a word to Pa about helicopter grandparenting. It was time for her to fly the nest.

Once Pa left in the shiny yellow hatchback, Arianne turned her full focus on Matt. She'd been fully aware of him the whole time.

"I'm so proud of you, Ari. You transferred from the car to your chair like a pro."

"That's what the workshops were about. It feels good to have another step of independence."

Matt stopped by his truck. "Can I be honest with you?" His eyes were shining with ... with what? Worry?

"I hope you'll be honest." A small twist of angst gripped her insides. Was he about to admit he'd thought better of developing something with her?

"I miss being able to pick you up."

"Why?"

"It was a great excuse to get close." He tested a grin.

"Do you need an excuse?" The butterflies were warming up their wings ready to soar.

"Well, yeah. Right at this moment, we're still just friends."

Arianne felt a lump of lead squash the butterflies. "Just friends. Is that what this is?"

"No!" Blood rushed to his cheeks. "Ari, I'm completely hopeless at saying the right thing at the right time. Can you give me some time to get it right? I'm gonna stop talking now. Let's get in my truck and go where we're going."

"Can I ask where we're going?"

"No." He grinned at her again. "How will you manage transferring to my truck cab?"

"Well I could try it, but then I wouldn't have an excuse." She winked at him and the blood rushed back to his cheeks.

The process was second nature now. Parking the wheelchair at the right angle, pulling the footrests up, Matt opening the door. But when he lifted her upright, her arms around his neck, this wasn't the same as before. He paused and caught her gaze for a moment. The pull to close the gap between her lips and his was strong, but despite the surge of warm emotion he held his position and grinned instead.

"Soon," he said. "I've got something to say first."

Impatience leaped out and jarred her teeth. *Just say it.*

But he didn't say anything while scooping her into his arms and placing her in the passenger seat, as he'd done many times before.

Silence reigned as Matt drove. To say it was a comfortable silence wouldn't have been accurate. It was full of anticipation, but it wasn't comfortable. The butterflies had turned up with tambourines and sparklers and were fixing to cause a riot.

They didn't drive far—about ten minutes out towards Lake Other, near Camp Trinity.

"There's a private spot out here. Joel Manning told me about it. Great for a picnic." Matt indicated his intention to turn off the main road. Arianne cast her caution aside and was turned slightly so she could watch him as he drove.

"You're watching me," Matt said.

"I am." Arianne was unrepentant. She saw his face redden. "It's an interesting outlook from where I'm sitting."

He grinned again as he started the drive along a short unpaved road to a small parking area near the lakefront.

Despite enjoying her study of Matthew Kennedy, her attention was drawn to where they were parking. "Wow. This is nice." There was plenty of daylight left, hardly a cloud in the sky, and not another soul in sight. No grandparents. No kind sisters. No Heidi Glasson with selfie stick in hand. Just the two of them. Time to see where this "friendship" was destined to go.

"Did Lucy help you with this?" Arianne used gravity to transfer herself to her chair, watching as Matt unloaded a huge picnic basket and blanket.

"No. What a thing to say." He had a frown, but Arianne could detect a smile tugging the corners of his mouth.

"Really?" She should have apologized but couldn't help challenging the doubt.

"Well, she offered a few suggestions, but I made the arrangements myself."

"Impressive."

Matt led the way down a walking path. It wasn't paved, but the ground was hard-packed and smooth, so Arianne was able to wheel along. Once they reached the lakefront, there was a grassy area someone obviously mowed. Unless …

"Did you cut the grass?"

Matt turned a shy smile in her direction. "Yeah."

"Smooth, Mr. Kennedy. You're scoring points thick and fast."

"Not with my folks. They wanted to know why I couldn't cut the grass at home."

Arianne laughed as Matt flung the blanket out. He turned toward her but she held up her hand.

"I've got another trick I want to show you." She wheeled over to the edge of the blanket, applied the brake, put her footrests up, then leaned forward, placing her left fisted hand on the blanket, her arm locked and strong, then swung herself from the chair onto the ground, bringing in the other arm to balance and stabilize. She lifted each of her legs and set them in a cross-legged pose. "What do you think?"

"Other than the fact I've lost another excuse?"

Arianne laughed again.

"It's amazing." He sat down next to her. "We could eat, or …"

"Or?" Arianne's heart missed two beats.

"Or I could try to tell you what's on my mind."

"What's on your mind?"

"Can I hold your hand?" He held out his hand in invitation. Arianne placed her hand in his, but the distance was too great. Matt shuffled to be closer, so close their shoulders touched. He tucked her arm under his and deftly entwined their fingers.

"Your actions are telling me something," Arianne said. "Do you have any words to add?"

Matt took a deep breath. "I want to develop our friendship to something more but I've hesitated because I'm scared of hurting you. I made a mess of it to start with, but you've been so kind and gracious. Thank you."

"I'd like to develop our friendship to something more as well, and, yes, I'm a bit scared of being hurt. Gavin undermined my trust something awful."

"I know. So can I talk openly?"

"We have to, or we can't move forward."

"I wanted to talk to you about this the day you capsized in the lake, but I'm always too slow getting my thoughts together."

"And I thought you had something going on with Heidi."

"Yeah. That's not likely. But she's hard to put off."

"So I saw on Heidi's World." She squeezed his hand and bumped his shoulder.

"You are a person living with disability …"

"That's true."

"And you do it with such grace, you put me to shame."

"You do okay. At least you're honest with yourself and open to learn."

"I am now. Jeanette fired so many rockets at me in the early days, I had to learn to keep my job."

"I love Jeanette."

"Well, so do I. If she hadn't forced me to get my head together, I wouldn't have noticed how amazing and beautiful you are."

Arianne smiled as warmth climbed into her throat. "Thank you."

"The point is, I was afraid to just go out with you because I knew if I took one step, I'd have to go the whole nine yards. I wasn't prepared to try a relationship out and then ditch it if I couldn't handle it."

"How do you know if you can handle it?" The old caution crept up.

"I don't. But I've come to the point of knowing I want to have a relationship with you. If I can't handle it, then I'll learn how. Besides, you might not be able to handle me."

Arianne grinned and bumped his shoulder again. "I think I'll manage."

"So can we go forward?" Matt held her gaze.

"Depends."

"On what?" He looked alarmed.

"On how well you kiss."

Matt grinned and then placed his free hand on the side of Arianne's face.

"You good to try?"

"Yes, sir. I'm good to try." The butterflies had a full marching band out now. Arianne melted into Matt's warm hand and allowed him to guide her face close to his until the gap was finally closed and his warm lips merged with hers. All caution was thrown to the wind, and she yielded to the connection that was happening as her heart opened completely.

———

Wow. Just wow. There was no going backward from here. Arianne Rayne was intoxicating. His heart was completely hers, and he wished they could continue this powerful physical connection, but it was best they refocused. It was all Matthew could do to turn his focus to the magnificent hamper Leah had put together for them.

"We better eat," he said.

"Yeah. I guess we better." She flashed a million-kilowatt smile at him.

She was so beautiful, and he swooped in for another kiss, though he deliberately made it quick.

"Food, Miss Rayne. We must eat food." He used all his willpower to pull away and open the hamper.

"This food is so good," Arianne said, as she finished the last bite of the Italian bruschetta with the fresh tomato, garlic, and basil topping. "Did you choose the menu?"

"I let Leah guide me. But she's done a good job." The sparkling organic apple juice rolled nicely from the real crystal glasses that Leah had packed in the hamper.

The food was good, and they focused on consuming it, commenting about the healthy quinoa and chicken salad with lime, ginger and chili dressing. But it wasn't the food that Matthew had foremost in his mind. Once they'd finished Becky's vanilla slices, it was time to get back to the business at hand—their new relationship.

Arianne helped Matthew pack the plates and glasses back in the hamper, and he put it aside. The sun dipped low in the sky and twilight was turning the sky to a beautiful clear navy blue.

"Would you like to do some star gazing?" Matthew asked.

"Absolutely. It would be a shame to waste such a gorgeous evening by going indoors." Arianne lifted her legs out and shuffled forward so she could lie on her back.

Matthew lay next to her, took her hand in his, and held it to his chest. "I used to do a lot of camping under the stars with my mates from school when we lived in the outback."

"Tell me about it. Your years in Australia, I mean." Arianne snuggled closer.

"I love Trinity Lakes, but there's a part of me that will always be Australian. Night skies in the outback are probably a bit like night skies in Texas. I've never been to Texas, but that's what I've heard."

"We lived in Texas for a few years when Dad worked in Dallas," Arianne said. "But Dallas was hardly the place for stargazing.

"My brother, Caleb, is getting married next January. He's asked the family to fly Down Under for the wedding."

Arianne rolled onto her side, and he turned to meet her gaze.

"That will be such a great opportunity for you. I'm jealous already."

He brought their joined hands up and kissed her knuckles. "Would you like to come?" The words just popped out of his mouth. Their relationship as a couple was brand new, and it was probably too soon to make such an invitation, but it seemed right.

"I'd love to." Arianne's smile lit her face.

"Would it be difficult flying internationally?"

"I've never flown internationally and my whole life is difficult, but I've gotten used to it. I can confidently say I can make whatever adaptations I need to make. Do you mean it?"

"Of course. I wanted to ask you as soon as Caleb told me about it this afternoon."

"Will your family mind having an interloper along?"

"You're hardly an interloper. As soon as I get home, I'm telling them about our new status."

"What exactly is our new status?"

Arianne sure liked to have her facts straight.

"I guess boyfriend-girlfriend at this stage. That's what I'll be saying, but ..."

"But?"

"Unless you hate it, I'm planning on a future together."

Arianne's face was a picture of serious question.

"Is that okay?" Matthew's mouth had gone dry.

She nodded. "It's more than okay, but you might have to be a bit patient with me. That was where Gavin and I were headed before the accident, and he bailed when things got tough. I guess I'm still a little gun-shy."

"I understand. Let's just be an item for a while and see what happens later."

"I'm still keen to go to Australia. Count me in, if it's okay with your folks."

"They'll love the idea." Matthew's head was close enough to easily close the distance, and when their lips met again, all the stars in the galaxy burst into light.

CHAPTER 17

Five months later

Arianne glanced out of the plane window as they prepared to land in San Francisco. She had to lean across Matt, which gave him the opportunity to put his arm around her. Lucy leaned back in her seat to give Arianne a clear view.

"Are you excited to be coming home?" Matt spoke close to her ear.

"I only lived in San Fran for five years. I wouldn't call it home."

The lights of the city glowed in the darkness. It was less cold down in California, so they were arriving in a city that wasn't at the mercy of snow and ice.

"I'll be glad to see my family though." Arianne leaned back a little and kissed him on the cheek. "Thanks for coming with me."

Lucy rolled her eyes and turned her gaze out the window.

They'd taken a late afternoon flight from Walla Walla to San Francisco, having just had enough time to enjoy Christmas lunch with their respective families.

"So your dad's okay to drive us to the airport in a few days?" Matt had returned to his upright position as the plane thumped and shuddered onto the runway.

"Mom and Dad will both come. They'd like to meet the rest of your family." Arianne still had hold of Matt's hand.

"I can't wait to get on the flight to Australia. It's been over twelve years since we were last there." Lucy was also facing forward now.

"Thanks for coming with us, Lucy," Arianne said. "It's good having someone around in case I need assistance."

"What am I?" Matt's tone feigned hurt.

"Someone who's not allowed in female bathrooms." Arianne bumped his shoulder. "I'm really glad to have you both here."

The seatbelt light went off, but Arianne didn't move. She remembered the drill. Passengers without disability disembarked first, then the cabin crew would bring the airline wheelchair.

"Where are your elbow-crutches?" Lucy asked.

"The cabin crew have stowed them safely somewhere. They'll bring them to me when we leave." Arianne had them on board in case she needed to use the bathroom. Thankfully, she hadn't. But would have to put her new skill of walking into practice on the long-haul flight to Sydney. It had been several months of targeted physical therapy and practice, but she was getting about. To say she was walking might have been a stretch, but her legs were giving her some support, and she was able to make them move along. The walking frame was easier to use than crutches, but too bulky for the aircraft.

Once they'd disembarked and picked up all their luggage, Arianne chose her faithful wheelchair. Of all the mobility aids, this was the fastest way to get about.

"Stand by, guys. My parents are approaching at one o'clock." Arianne watched as her father—a younger version of Pa—and mother drew near.

"I thought you said you were walking again." Mom's greeting was completely as expected.

"How are you, Mom? Dad? This is my boyfriend, Matt, and his sister, Lucy." Arianne ignored Mom's greeting, determined to direct the conversation onto positive ground.

"Merry Christmas." Matt shook Dad's hand and received an air-kiss from Mom. "Thanks for having us."

"Merry Christmas to you, too," Dad said. "Thanks for bringing our girl home."

Arianne caught Lucy's worried expression and gave her a sly wink, followed by a grin. She mouthed "don't worry," and gave a small shake of her head.

Mom came around behind as if to start pushing Arianne. A deep breath. "I'm fine, Mom. Just walk beside me and tell me how your Christmas has been so far."

Mom cast a confused glance toward Dad.

"She's fine, Sylvia."

And just like that, the past nine months of living in Trinity Lakes made perfect sense. She'd always known it, but her mother's cosseting negativity was a stark contrast to Gran and Pa.

Even Dad was surprised when Matt opened the car door and allowed Arianne to transfer herself into the front passenger seat. Her shoulder and legs had strengthened enough that she could do it without the slide board.

"Wow, Arianne. You've come a long way since March." Dad got into the driver's seat.

"I'm just getting warmed up." Arianne grinned at him.

Traffic was almost non-existent, and they got back to the house in under half an hour. It was getting late, but not so late that there wasn't time for an eggnog and exchange of presents.

"By the way, Ari, I've let some of your friends know you're in town for a few days. They may visit." Mom dropped the comment calmly as she opened her Christmas present, but Arianne felt her gut twist. She hadn't seen her friends since she'd railed at them. She couldn't remember exactly what she'd said but knew she'd thrown harsh cutting words at them. Her state of grief and depression at the time were definitely a factor in the display, but Arianne had hurt her friends, and hadn't had the courage to speak to them since.

"You okay?" Matt whispered in her ear.

Arianne forced a smile that was probably more like a grimace. "I'll be okay. God is just giving me another opportunity to mend some bridges."

"You'll be great." Matt pulled Arianne into a warm snuggle. It was so good having him there as a support. He'd really learned how to read her, and it felt good.

After two days staying with her parents, Arianne was glad she lived in Trinity Lakes. She loved Mom, but Mom's never-ending critical outlook was a strain. Trying to stay positive and focused on good relationships was hard work.

"Will you be okay going out on your own?" Arianne watched as Matt and Lucy got their jackets and bags and phones.

"The question is, will you be okay here on *your* own?" Matt came across and kissed her on the forehead.

"I need to see these friends. Last time we spoke … well, we didn't speak. I was an unhappy emotional wreck, and caring about how they felt wasn't at the top of my priorities. I'll be good. What are you guys going to do?"

"We've booked a day tour around Alcatraz. Have you been there?"

"Yeah. We did a field trip my senior year of high school."

"I'm praying you have a good time with your friends." Lucy gave Arianne a hug.

"Thanks, Lucy. Have a great day with your brother. I'm jealous." She smiled as Matt approached.

"None of this crouchy huggy thing." He held out his arms and she took hold to hoist herself to standing position, from where they could enjoy a proper embrace and kiss. "I love you," Matt said.

It wasn't the first time he'd said it, but it never got old. "I love you, too. Don't stay out too long."

"Yes, dear." He pecked another kiss, then guided her back to the wheelchair.

The hour until her friends had arranged to visit ticked by slowly, and Arianne went over and over again how she wanted to greet them.

"I'm so so sorry about the way I treated you last time we spoke." Arianne gushed the moment Chelsea and Zoe walked through the living room door. "I was horrible, and I know it must have hurt you."

The usual long-time-no-see chit chat was struck off the list. Both young women descended on Arianne, throwing their arms around her, sobbing. It was cathartic, the tears and apologies. When they'd finally calmed, they sat together and drank coffee, which Arianne insisted on making for them.

"I'm so glad to see you doing so well," Zoe said. "Your Mom said something about you walking again."

Arianne felt a stab of worry. Her Mom was always saying things that weren't the complete truth. "Yes, technically. But I need these." She produced the elbow-crutches stowed on the back of her chair, fitted them on her arms, and pushed herself to standing. She did a small turn about the living room, putting superhuman effort into making each foot shuffle forward. She could do it, albeit slowly. When she returned to her chair, she saw the looks on her friends' faces.

"Guys. This is good news, really. They doubted I'd ever walk again. Being able to do a few steps here and there is great."

Chelsea tested a smile. "Sorry, Ari. I guess your mom expected more, but I'm happy for you. So long as you're happy."

"I am. I'm really happy. Did Mom tell you I have a boyfriend?"

The puzzled looks had a hint of panic attached.

"What?" Arianne asked. "I do have a boyfriend. He and his sister are out sightseeing today, but I'm going with them to Australia for their brother's wedding in two days' time."

Chelsea exchanged a look with Zoe.

"What?" Arianne could see there was something. "What's the matter?"

"Didn't your mom tell you?"

"Tell me what?" Her gut tightened.

"Gavin is coming to see you later."

Gavin. There was a name that would ruin every party. Except God had done a miracle in her heart where Gavin was concerned. She didn't hate him. Wasn't even angry with him anymore. But did she want to see him? That was another question entirely.

"Do you want us to stay while he visits?" The concern on Zoe's face made Arianne want to hug her again.

"I'm not sure." The thoughts and feelings were rushing around Arianne's head, dive-bombing her heart, and springing back up with anxiety attached. Deep breath.

Chelsea reached for her phone. "Do you want us to call him and tell him to not come?"

Deep breath. Focus. Remember the night when you received prayer, and the Holy Spirit brought waves of healing, joy, and strength.

"Ari?" Chelsea asked again.

"I'd really like your support when I face Gavin, but it's not fair on you. He's your friend as well."

"We haven't seen him much since he got out of prison," Zoe said. "He wasn't exactly open and friendly … you know…"

"Prison? I didn't know … was it because of …"

"You knew he was charged with vehicular assault, right?" Chelsea paled, as if she was worried about having spoken out of turn.

"No, I didn't know. Mom and Dad might have said something, but honestly, at the time, I was probably too tied up in my own grief to understand."

"It went to court. Didn't your folks tell you?"

Arianne rolled her lips together. They had arranged for her to talk to a lawyer, who'd prepared an affidavit. Was that because she couldn't appear as a witness? Was that for the court case? She chased her thoughts around. Had Gavin broken up with her before the court case, or after? It must have been before if he'd been given a prison sentence. Oh, man. This was a mess.

"I can call Gavin and tell him you're not ready to see him." Chelsea scrolled through her phone for his number.

"No. Chels. Wait. I need to see him. God helped me find forgiveness at Easter. I guess Gavin probably needs to forgive me as well, since he had to do time."

Chelsea looked at Zoe with a frown again.

"I don't think you should feel too sorry for him ..." Zoe stopped speaking when Arianne held up her hand.

"This is not about feeling sorry for him. This is about me being completely free of him. I don't want there to be anything between us anymore, not even anger. I need to talk to him."

"Do you want us to stay?" Zoe said.

What she really wanted was for Matt to come back and be with her, but they were booked for the day outing. She wasn't going to call them back.

"I'll be okay. But thanks. It's been so good seeing you again, and I hope that you can come and see us up at Trinity Lakes sometime. Come for a vacation or something. It's a beautiful place, and I know someone who owns a bed-and-breakfast on the lake."

———

Arianne didn't know whether to be thankful or annoyed her mother had arranged for Gavin to visit. One thing was for certain, Arianne would not ever have made the arrangement herself. Was this an opportunity for another step of healing? She hoped so. And with Matt and Lucy unreachable for the day, it was also an opportunity for Arianne to search deep in her heart for God's strength, grace, and wisdom.

Once the girls had left, Arianne sought out her mother. "Thanks for the heads-up about Gavin coming around."

Her mother's head swung around, and there was no mistaking the look of guilt on her face. "You and he were meant to be together. Now you're doing so much better, I thought it was time you talked things out."

"Mom. Really?" Arianne's voice rose in frustration, despite her determination to stay calm. "Did you not understand when I introduced you to Matt that he's the one I am seeking a future with?"

"You have unresolved issues with Gavin."

"That we can agree on." Arianne wheeled over to the kitchen table. "But you cannot think for a moment that I want to renew things with Gavin."

Mom's eyes searched every direction of the room except Arianne's.

"Mom." Arianne injected a no-nonsense into her words. "Do you understand?"

There were a few beats of strained silence as Arianne waited for her mother to respond.

"Just give him a chance, Arianne. He's been through a tough time."

The temptation to explode was pushing from every which way, but Arianne took yet another deep breath and turned her thoughts back to the night at the healing meeting.

"I will give him the chance to apologize, and I will apologize to him, and that will be all. Please don't hope for more, because it's not going to happen."

The doorbell rang, and Mom's eyes lit up with hope. "That will be him. I'll get the door. You go into the living room."

Mom left the room and Arianne fought not to pout like a teenager. It didn't matter anyway. What she had to say to Gavin would be just between them. Her mother wouldn't stay in the room.

"Here she is." Mom opened the door that led from the hallway to the living room and ushered Gavin inside. Arianne's heart stopped for a split second. Gavin walked in, some pounds lighter than when she'd seen him last, and with a visible scar over his right eyebrow. Was that from the accident? She couldn't remember. The last time she'd seen him, he'd pulled the last shred of hope from her life. That, on top of the prospect of permanent disability, had been perhaps the lowest point of her life.

"Do you want a coffee?" Mom's question penetrated Arianne's daze.

"Sure. Thanks." Gavin's voice was the same smooth, deep tone.

"Sit down." Mom waved toward the couch. "Ari?"

"Thanks, Mom. We'll be fine. Would you give us some time, please?" Thankfully, Mom closed the door as she went into the kitchen.

A strange silence descended. What was he thinking? Arianne couldn't read his expression.

Eventually, Gavin took a deep breath through his nose. "I expected to see you walking. Your Mom said ..."

"My Mom often paints pictures that might not reveal all the details."

"So, you're still ..." He waved his hand toward her seated in her chair.

"Still ... what?" Arianne wasn't going to make this easy, even though she heard the whisper of the Holy Spirit in the back of her mind to show grace.

"Well, I thought ... anyway ... Your mom said you were walking again."

Arianne pulled her elbow crutches around, fitted them and then pushed herself upright. She took the faltering steps and seated herself on the sofa opposite Gavin. The look on his face said it all. This wasn't what he'd expected.

"How have you been, Gavin?" Arianne decided to move the conversation along.

"Since having had to serve four months in prison, you mean?"

Wow. Was that accusation in his tone?

"I only heard you were sentenced this morning. How was that?"

"How do you think, Ari? It was awful, and all thanks to you."

So this meeting wasn't about reconciliation, as her mother had hoped, but about accusation. Great.

"I'm sorry you lost those four months. How have you found things since getting out?"

"Not particularly easy, if you must know. I don't know why you had to tell them I was speeding."

Grace. Patience. Wisdom. *Lord, I need you now.*

"I just answered the questions they asked."

"Perhaps you could have thought about how that would turn out for me."

"I wasn't thinking about you at the time. You're right. I'm sorry."

Gavin relaxed back on his chair, but the look on his face was still petulant.

"You'll be pleased to know I'm now settled in Trinity Lakes." Arianne refused to let the atmosphere go dark. "I've recently bought a car, got a job at a gym, and tomorrow I'm taking a trip to Australia for a wedding."

Gavin frowned. "It looks like it's all worked out nicely for you, hasn't it?"

"I'm happy, Gavin. I've adjusted to living with a disability, and I'm getting on with taking every opportunity that comes my way."

"So you don't see a future for us?"

Was he kidding?

"You broke up with me, Gavin. You said you couldn't cope. That this was not what you'd signed up for." She gestured toward the wheelchair.

"I was angry when I found out you'd made a statement to the cops."

"We all had to make statements. It's the law."

His jaw tensed and eyes narrowed as he processed her words.

"I'm sorry I broke up with you," he eventually said. "I should have been more supportive."

You think? Arianne wished she could have said that aloud but knew it would provoke him.

"Well, I'm pleased to tell you that I had a spiritual healing early in the year, and I've forgiven you." She tested a smile in his direction.

"You've forgiven me? What for?"

Oh, this man was priceless. And clueless.

"It doesn't matter, Gavin. All you need to know is that it's all good between us. I'm happy to let it go."

"So you want to get back together?"

What had she ever seen in him?

"I think my boyfriend might object."

"Boyfriend?"

"Yes. I'm traveling with him and his family to his brother's wedding in Australia. I think I mentioned it."

"You didn't mention a boyfriend."

"My apologies. He and his sister are out sightseeing today,

but they'll be back soon. Do you want to hang around and meet him?"

"Ah. No thanks. I think if we've cleared the air, I'd better be on my way." He stood up and straightened his jacket.

Arianne had a sudden conviction of guilt. She hadn't been very kind.

"Gavin, I'm honestly sorry you had to serve a prison sentence. I pray you can pick up your life and move forward from here." She hoisted herself from the sofa and shuffled toward the door.

"I guess I'm sorry, too, Arianne. It was probably tough for you after the accident."

"It was." Arianne gave him a weak smile.

"I'm glad you've found a good life up north."

"Thanks, Gavin." She had the urge to hug him, but movement wasn't natural or easy, and it was awkward asking him to come closer, so she decided to let him go unhugged.

"Hope your boyfriend doesn't get mad knowing I dropped around."

"I will be telling him about it the moment he steps in the door. He'll be fine."

EPILOGUE

This was so beautiful. And hot. So different from January in the United States. Arianne sat next to Marianne and James Kennedy in the small stone church. Matt stood at the front as best man for his brother Caleb, looking ridiculously handsome in an open necked shirt with smart black trousers. It was too hot for full suits. The accessibility issue hadn't been addressed in this church, though Caleb said it was now on the top of his list of things to do once he got back from his honeymoon. Still, she'd managed to get inside with her elbow-crutches and was watching this beautiful wedding.

Lucy was a bridesmaid, and wore a shoestring strapped deep olive-green satin three-quarter length dress with a scooped neckline. Despite the outside temperature of nearly a hundred degrees, the folks inside the church were dressed to celebrate this joyful day.

Arianne loved being with the Kennedy family. Matt had taken her on a tour of all his haunts from when he was in high school, and it was funny to hear how his accent had morphed once they were talking with the locals.

"Can't help it," he'd said. "My formative years were spent speaking Aussie slang. What can you do?"

Arianne smiled as she heard that same Aussie accent spoken by the officiating minister and as Alanah and Caleb exchanged vows. Though she could tell Caleb was American, his accent had definite traces of Australian as well.

Once the bride and groom had exited the church, Matt came back to make sure Arianne was able to exit without falling down the three stone steps at the front.

"You look gorgeous," he said to her as she got to the door.

"You look pretty sharp yourself." She smiled back at him.

"Do you mind if I just lift you down these steps and save us the drama?"

"I was hoping you'd ask. It's a great excuse." She winked at him and he swept her up in his arms.

Before depositing her in the chair waiting at the bottom of the steps, she stole a kiss.

"Couldn't resist it," she said. He smiled back.

"We're going to take some photos here outside the church before we head off to the hall for the reception."

"No worries." Arianne wheeled herself to a place where she could watch the photos being shot. Alanah and Caleb were obviously madly in love. They couldn't stop kissing each other.

Once they'd taken all the pictures with Alanah's family, the Walkers, Caleb called for his own tribe to assemble.

"Are you coming?" Matt held out his hand to Arianne.

"Me?" She saw that everyone was watching, waiting. "But this is your family."

"Right." Matt grinned at her, then helped her to stand upright. "Did I mention that I was hoping you'd join the Kennedy family. Like permanently?"

Though she was in the circle of his arms, she drew back and searched his gaze with a small frown in place.

"What are you saying?"

"Will you marry me? Please. That is, if you want to?"

If she wanted to? What a silly question. There were a host of party-popping beans stirring in her stomach.

"Did you just propose to me in front of your family, while they're patiently waiting for us?"

He grinned. "I think so. Yes. Will you?"

She smiled back, then leaned forward and initiated a warm and loving kiss.

"Hurry up, Matt!" Lucy called.

"Can't tell them now," Matt said. "This is Caleb and Alanah's day."

Arianne nodded. "Of course. So am I still welcome in the family photo?"

"Are you coming?" Sasha called this time.

"Come on. Time for you to join our family." Matt handed Arianne her crutches. Together they moved into position, just next to Lucy.

"So she said 'yes'?" Lucy cast Arianne a sly grin.

"She said yes." Matt slipped his arm around Arianne's waist and kissed her cheek. "And made me the happiest man today."

"Tomorrow," Arianne said. "Caleb is the happiest today. Your turn tomorrow."

BEFORE YOU GO:

If you enjoyed this story, would you mind taking a few minutes to pop a review on the site where you purchased *Over the Rainbow*, or on the Good Reads website. Every review helps me, as an author, to get new readers involved. Thank you for spending the time with me, the team of authors in this series and the population of Trinity Lakes.

Meredith

AUTHOR NOTES

The testimony of Chrys Webb, shared as a part of the healing service, is a true story Chrys shared with me. Though this healing occurred in the early 1980s, Chrys has never had any return of the MS. She and her husband went on to become pastors and have served in several churches in South Australia.

In the scene where Arianne experiences the healing power of God's love, I've mentioned two songs: "Trust in You" by Lauren Daigle and "The Hurt and The Healer" by Mercy Me. Both songs are powerful. If you are in a place like Arianne, I encourage you to listen to the songs and let the spirit of healing minister to you through the words and music.

In the scene where Arianne talked to Gran about inspirational quotes, I mentioned two people whose amazing stories have encouraged many people living with disability. In this You Tube clip, Nick Vujicic reunites with Joni Eareckson Tada, two of the most well-known advocates for people living with disability, and preachers of the gospel of Jesus Christ, chat about the initiative, Champions for the Disabled.

ALSO IN THE TRINITY LAKES ROMANCE SERIES

Tangled up in Love

Book #9 Trinity Lakes Romance
By Carolyn Miller

One kiss didn't mean much. One kiss could mean everything.

When Ellie Reilly returns from a dream overseas trip, a too-long hug from her best friend Jasper Cohen clues her in that his feelings might be more than what she suspected. He's unsure about pushing their friendship further, and doubly uncertain when her European friend, Sebastian, seeks her out in Trinity Lakes.

Uncertainty is something Ellie knows all too well. Since returning from her vacation, Ellie feels like she doesn't fit at her family's ranch or in small town life. When she is asked to take on responsibility for reopening Trinity Lakes' historical museum - a dream she's always wanted - she can't help but wonder if settling for life in the familiar is all that God has for her, or can she dare trust Him for more?

Can these two best friends push past mistakes and insecurities and find a future together?

A friends-to-more, small town contemporary Christian romance. Book five of the Trinity Lakes Romance series (can be read as a standalone). Visit Trinity Lakes and meet the fun and quirky characters who value family, faith, and happily-ever-afters.

Don't miss the earlier titles in the series:

Never Find Another You by Narelle Atkins
The Ocean Between Us by Meredith Resce
Love Somebody Like You by Carolyn Miller
Where Our Hearts Lie by Jenny Glazebrook
No Matter How Far by Sara Beth Williams
I'll Always Choose You by Lisa Renee
Always by My Side by Iola Goulton

ALSO BY MEREDITH RESCE

Book #1 Luella Linley – License to Meddle series

Organized Backup

Regency romance author, Luella Linley, arranges her characters' lives, making sure that they weather all storms and live happily-ever-after. Her characters are putty in her hands, but her 21st Century adult children are not so easily organized. When her daughter, Megan, asks for support with an inappropriate situation at work, Luella decides Megan should get a boyfriend to intimidate her boss. The cop who just pulled Luella over for speeding is a likely candidate.

Cam Fletcher is expecting to be interviewed by a famous author. Instead of sharing insights into his job working in the police force, he is sharing a meal with the famous author and her daughter, Megan. When left alone with Megan, Cam wonders when the interview will begin. The parents' extended absence gives him a clue, which Megan confirms. Luella Linley is playing matchmaker, but is he willing to play the game.

Book#2 Luella Linley – License to Meddle series

In Want of a Wife

Can she hit the target twice in a row? Luella Linley can't resist the opportunity to show her daughter's picture to the handsome lawyer. What can it hurt? But Chloe is not amused at her mother's attempts to matchmake … except the man is a lawyer, and she has an unjust speeding ticket she wants to fight in court.

Book #3 in Luella Linley – License to Meddle series

All Arranged

by Meredith Resce

Luella Linley should feel satisfied that she has been instrumental in getting her two daughters happily settled. Her meddling was successful, but came at a price, and husband, Russell, has advised she leave the children to their own devices.

But her eldest, Pete, is thirty-five, living back at home and discouraged. His fiancée left him days before the planned wedding and six months on, Pete still hasn't recovered. Louise might be biased, but her responsible, hard-working and handsome son would make a good husband and father—but he's given up after three failed relationships. He is a good catch, but unlikely to be fooled by his mother's scheming and meddling as she did with his sisters.

This situation calls for something special. A direct approach. Just like in her novels. Let the parents do the arranging and sort out the wheat from the chaff. This method will take any risk of rejection out of the equation, and let's face it, a mother can tell what's needed for a successful long-term relationship.

Carrie Davis dedicated herself to her career long ago. Her one and only serious relationship was a disaster, put down mainly to her youthful naivety at the time. Up until the birth of her niece, Carrie had not considered that she might even like a relationship, but now thoughts of loneliness are stalking her. Carrie's sister, Ellen, knows and when she sees an odd advert in the classified ads, she begins to wonder if this is a prank or an opportunity sent from heaven. "Wanted. For a social experiment. A family arranged marriage."

ABOUT THE AUTHOR

South Australian Author, Meredith Resce, has been writing since 1991, and has had books in the Australian market since 1997.

Following the Australian success of her *Heart of Green Valley* series, they were released in the UK.

Over the Rainbow is Meredith's 25th published title.

Apart from writing, Meredith teaches high school students. She is an avid reader, particularly Christian fiction. She is a fan of British costume-drama television series, and British cosy mystery shows. Jane Austen, L.M. Montgomery and Charles Dickens are favorite classic authors. Meredith is a country-girl at heart, and takes every opportunity to visit the farm where she grew-up.

Aussie rules football and cricket are her choice when following televised sport. Come on Aussies!

Meredith often speaks to groups on issues relevant to relationships and emotional and spiritual growth.

Meredith has also been co-writer and co-producer in the 2007 feature film production, *Twin Rivers* now available on streaming.

With her husband, Nick, Meredith has worked in Christian ministry since 1983.

Meredith and Nick have three adult children.

To find out more about Meredith Resce and subscribe to her newsletter.

https://meredithresce.com/join-our-mailing-list-and-stay-connected/

www.meredithresce.com

www.facebook.com/MeredithResceAuthor